ACE

A Christmas To Remember

A Novella for Ace

Steel Patriots MC

Book 8

Mary Kennedy

TABLE OF CONTENTS

A Christmas To Remember

CHAPTER ONE

The police cars were loud, their lights flashing in the darkness like a laser show. The long red fire trucks hummed, their engines still running, the firemen scary in their big coats and helmets. Alex had never seen so many people in his short life. In fact, he'd rarely seen people other than those his foster parents allowed into the home to torture him through his cage. A cage nestled inside a large closet with nothing but a bucket for his human waste, a small blanket to cover his body at night, and a sliver of light from the doorway.

It wasn't until the people showed up today that he discovered not all children were kept in cages in a closet or made fun of by other adults. It wasn't until today that he knew he was small for his age, malnourished, he heard someone say. It wasn't until today that he knew kindness existed in people bigger than himself.

Sgt. John Mills was a big man; the biggest man he'd ever seen with a barrel chest and salt-and-pepper hair. He had a kind smile and giant gentle hands. He'd lifted Alex from the cage, wrapping him in a blanket, hugging him close to that big chest. It was the first hug Alex could remember ever receiving in his young life. He settled him in the seat of his car, handing him a small bear from his trunk. Alex looked at it and wondered what he was supposed to do with it.

Sgt. Mills spoke to a woman outside the car, but he couldn't hear what they were saying. There was so much happening, and it was loud and chaotic. Opening the door, Sgt. Mills knelt beside him, giving him the friendliest smile Alex had ever seen.

"Hi, Alex, remember me? I'm Sgt. John Mills, the man who wrapped you up and got you out of that closet. This lady is Mrs. Williams with Child Protective Services. No one here is going to hurt you, okay?" He nodded his little head, the huge blue eyes seemingly too big for his gaunt, pale face.

"Alex," said the big man, "I know this is really scary for you, but I want to make sure you're taken care of, and well, I was wondering if you might like to come home with me?"

"In... in a cage?" he asked quietly. John Mills' fists clenched and unclenched, even Mrs. Williams looked away from him.

"No, son, you will never be in a cage again. You will have your own room, your own toys and books, your own bed, everything. We're going to make sure you get lots to eat and make you the big boy you should be. When you're ready, we'll get you enrolled in school."

"W-with other kids?" he asked.

"Yes, son, with other children. For now, I'll be your foster dad, but I can tell you, Alex, I'd really like to adopt you one day if you think you might like that." The little boy looked at the woman and back at the kind man, then nodded.

"Sgt. Mills, you know that I'm breaking the rules in allowing you to do this," said the woman.

"I know, I know, but I can't let that boy go back into the system, not after this. I'm gonna take him to the emergency room and get him taken care of. I'll take some leave to get him settled in, and when the time is right, I'll adopt him. I promise you that I will get him all the care he needs, all the tutors, counselors, anything. I don't have children of my own, you know that, and I want this boy to have a fighting chance."

"Alright, John," she said sympathetically, "I understand, really, I do. It's going to be a long road, John. You have no idea what all has been done to that boy. A long, long road."

It was a long road indeed but one that John Mills never regretted taking.

That first night at home, John allowed the boy to take a bubble bath, one that turned into an hour-long adventure for the boy, playing with a small toy boat he'd picked up at the drug store. When he fixed him a sandwich and some soup, he'd barely eaten three bites claiming he was full. He wasn't full. It was just that his stomach was so small it couldn't tolerate any more food. He read him three books that night and tucked him into the bed, leaving a light on for him.

An hour later, as he checked on the boy in the room, he noticed he was no longer in the bed. A trend that would continue.

For those first few weeks, John would wake up and hear the whimpering of the little boy and find him curled in the closet beneath blankets, hiding from imaginary hands stretching out to touch him. Despite his many attempts, he couldn't convince him it was safe to come out, so instead, he would crawl in there with him and just lie next to him, talking about the stars and the moon, the county fair, anything to get his mind off his terrors.

Within three months, he was finally sleeping in his own bed and had gained nearly fifteen pounds. By the end of the year, he was in school and excelling in every subject. Although Alex was highly uncomfortable with touch, he wasn't diagnosed with any form of autism, instead believing that it stemmed from his traumatic childhood.

But John Mills never pushed the boy to do more than he was capable of or prepared for. He would lay a hand on his shoulder only briefly or touch his hand but never lingered, knowing the touch would hurt him. When Alex wanted to get involved in sports, John knew that contact sports would not be the way to go, so instead, he enrolled him in swimming and cross-country.

It was the perfect thing for young Alex. By the time he graduated from high school a year early, he knew that going to college would be challenging for him. Enrolling in online courses, he also knew that he needed to further himself. He'd spent his youth hearing the tales of his adoptive father in the Navy and desperately wanted to join; however, the recruiters weren't so sure. That is until they received his aptitude scores and his ideas around security and intelligence. Then they knew that Alex Mills would be a gem for their records.

At his naval graduation, he stood proudly in his uniform, staring

into the stands at the only man who had ever believed in him, ever loved

him. Now he needed to do something that would prove he was worthy.

Now he would find a way to save others.

CHAPTER TWO

Alex "Ace" Mills, United States Navy Intelligence Officer, officially assigned to Special Forces Command, listened to the intelligence being sent to his team and cringed.

What the hell is this guy doing?

Normally assigned to the joint special forces team run by Eric "Ghost" Stanton, Ace was pulled to work on a special assignment with the joint chiefs on a remote base, far removed from his team. He didn't understand it, nor did he understand why they even needed him. Someone with lesser skills and lesser seniority could easily do what he'd been tasked to do.

His ears perked up as he heard the casual way in which his replacement was feeding the information. Damn! What was he thinking? This idiot couldn't fight his way out of a paper bag. Inside his sanctuary, his small computer office, he knew that no one else could enter without knocking. It was his own personal rule, and for the most part, everyone complied. Hitting a few keystrokes, he was in the backdoor to the computer on the other end.

"Seriously? He's playing Warcraft. Holy shit," he whispered to himself. Fine, he can play his games, thought Ace. I'll spoon-feed the bastard the information.

Doing what he did best, he started digging, finding every piece of information he could on the alleged kidnappers, except what he discovered indicated it wasn't a kidnapping. It was pure and simple terrorism. The girls wouldn't make it out alive if they weren't found soon.

Ace followed the trail of information, firing off anonymous bits of information to the man on the other end of the line, waiting patiently to see if he would forward the information to his team. Why wasn't this guy doing his damn job?

Hearing the communication that the girls were found dead, Ace let out a long slow breath and then took matters into his own hands, running the probabilities on where they may have gone. When he was finished, through a secure site, he fed Ghost the trail he believed the terrorists took and then sat back.

Non sibi sed patgriae. Not self but country. The unofficial motto for the Navy, but one that Ace liked. He recited the line over and over in his head, helping to calm his nerves, waiting patiently to hear if the team found the men. A knock on his door disrupted his thoughts, and he clicked off the secure line, turning to open the door.

"Sir," he said, standing at attention.

"Mills, we need you in the conference room," said Admiral Crossing. He looked at the computer screens behind Alex and squinted as if he would be able to read what was filtering across his monitors. Crossing would need to be not only adept at coding but also ciphering and hacking, which Alex knew he was not.

"Yes, sir," he said, turning to gather his trusty laptop. It would be five more days before he learned of the outcome of the mission. Five days to hear how they'd found those children hanging from a cliff, abused, raped, and beaten. Five days to hear how they'd tracked down the terrorists, tortured them, and then blown them into the wind with enough C4 to sink a ship.

It would be another sixty days before he heard that the team was being asked to retire. When Alex asked if he could retire with his team, the admiral told him he was too valuable and they couldn't allow him to leave at this time.

"Besides," said the admiral, "you weren't part of this clusterfuck, don't let it taint your record."

Clusterfuck? This was the other idiots cluster, not his team's.

A year later, after contacting Ghost, he decided to leave on his own terms. Nothing was what it seemed, and nothing could ever erase the betrayal he knew existed. His team had suffered because of the career aspirations of Admiral Crossing's inept nephew, and he couldn't bother to be near the man any longer.

Two months later, he knocked on the door of the Steel Patriots only to be greeted by a smiling Ghost and grinning Whiskey. The man desperately wanted to pull him in for a brotherly hug but instead satisfied with a loud clap or two, welcoming him to their newly formed team.

A new life, a life away from the Navy, away from everything that had become so familiar to him. Now, he was a Harley-riding, tattoo-wearing, badass biker, albeit with serious human contact issues.

He was back with his team, helping to save the little guy, providing intel, and finally feeling at home. Dad would be proud.

CHAPTER THREE

Ace's feet crunched in the snow along the trail they'd cleared just yesterday. Overnight flurries caused the trail to once more be blanketed in white. He didn't mind. In fact, it was one of his favorite things to do. Running in the snow, or cold in general, almost guaranteed him alone time.

After spending the last six years with the Steel Patriots, he'd learned a few things about himself. One, he was appreciated by the men he served with more than he ever thought possible. Two, he wasn't quite as dysfunctional as he'd allowed himself to believe all these years. Three, he could allow people to touch him; it just had to be the right people and the right circumstances.

It started with Grace, the wife of Ghost. When she'd shown up at their compound beaten and abused, he felt so sorry for her. He wanted to hold her hand the way Ghost did, but he just couldn't. What he could do, though, was what he did best. Track her ex-husband.

Then when Doc fell in love with Bree, that was an easy one for him as well. He not only tracked down her stepfather, but he also removed him from this planet. People often thought that because Ace was the computer geek in the room that he wasn't trained in the ways of the team. It was an underestimation that often played out well for Ace.

The truth was he was a black belt in six different disciplines of martial arts. He was weapons trained on anything the team used. He was fast, excelled in hand-to-hand, and had a keen sense of awareness to his surroundings. Underestimate him, and it wouldn't work out well for you.

Following Doc was Whiskey and Kat, then Zulu and Angel eyes, Gunner and Darby, Tango and Taylor, and then just recently Razor and Bella. His teammates found the women that completed their difficult worlds, and he couldn't be happier for them.

Each and every woman helped him to overcome his issues with touch, not sexually, but by simple gestures such as handholding or sitting closely with their legs touching. It all helped, and it all made a difference to Ace.

Their love and compassion toward him were something he didn't take lightly, nor did he ever believe he could pay back. That is until they started talking about their book club.

Grace possessed a serious devotion to romance novels, but particularly to romance novels with a lot of sex in them... a lot! She originally shared the books with the twins, although God knew why. Those two raging hormone, over-sexed men didn't need any help in that department.

When Bree came on board, Grace and she shared the books. Then it was Kat, an inexperienced young woman who wanted all the help she could find. Pretty soon, all of the women were reading the books of CC Robat and discussing them on a weekly, if not more frequently, basis.

When the men discovered why the sex was suddenly through the roof, they all started reading the books as well. A few nights ago, with the stack of books sitting on his nightstand, Ace decided to see what all the fuss was about. By the time he'd finished the first one, he was so painfully hard he had to take matters into his own hands.

After the fourth book, his dick was so raw from rubbing it, he thought it might fall off. Finding a woman willing to take care of it for him was difficult, to say the least. Not because of the way he looked; he knew that. At six-foot-one and one hundred and eighty pounds of lean muscle, his jet-black hair and blue eyes made him attractive to most women. What was harder was asking a woman to suck his dick without touching him.

Now, at least, he understood the fascination with the books and why his teammates were smiling more than usual.

Ace watched as the women flitted around the restaurant, preparing to put up the holiday decorations. He heard each of them discussing what they were going to get their spouses and, of course, what they would spoil the kids with this year. For Ace, it was a bittersweet moment to realize he didn't have anyone in his life to buy presents for. He would certainly get the kids each something as the favorite geek uncle, but his father was dead now, and he had no one in his life, nor was it likely he ever would.

He heard the women giggling about the latest chapter they'd read together, and he could only grin. Then it hit him. The gift that would be perfect for all of the adults. Opening his laptop, he started searching. Three hours later, frustrated that he could find nothing except a fan club address, he started typing.

Dear CC Robat,

My apologies for the lack of formality, but since I'm unsure of whether to say Mr. Robat or Ms./Miss/Mrs. Robat, I'm covering my bases.

You are a difficult person to find, and finding people is my job, so that's saying a lot.

My name is Alex Mills, and I'm a member of a motorcycle club called the Steel Patriots. I suppose I should back up just a bit.

I was a member of the United States Navy, part of Naval Intelligence supporting Special Forces overseas. My role was to extend critical information to my team to support them in missions, and I did. Unfortunately, during our last mission, I couldn't be with the team, and things didn't go as planned. But as with any team, we move as one, and they blamed me for nothing, trying to relieve me of the burden I felt for not having been there to support them.

My entire team retired, as did I a year later. Then we formed the motorcycle club. But we do more than just ride bikes. We help the underdogs; we rescue trafficked and abused women and children. We run a successful restaurant and bar, a custom motorcycle and auto shop, a clinic which supports our community, and so much more.

My teammates over the last two years have met the women they want to spend their lives with. They've married, had children, or will very soon. They've fallen in love and, in the process, changed my world. You see, although I am part of this amazing team, I am always somewhat on the periphery. By choice.

It's a rather sordid tale, but I don't do well with crowds or touching, so I usually sit at the edge. I'm getting better. I'm trying, but I see the relationships that my friends have, and it makes me very happy for them. Gunner, one of my teammates, is married to Darby. She owns the local bookstore.

You see, Grace, another wife, is crazy for your books. She buys them, shares them with the other wives, and they all discuss the... sex scenes. My teammates were so shocked by the changes in their wives. When they found out it was because of your books, they started reading them all as well.

So, all that to get to my point. I'd like you to come to Club Steel for Christmas. I know it's short notice and all, but if you could do a book signing at the Page Turner and then just spend the holiday with us, it would be extremely important to my teammates and their wives.

If you have your own family, obviously, they are invited as well. I am giving this gift to all of them so they can personally thank you, so I will cover all of your expenses. Tell me where you're flying from, and I can *book the ticket or simply reimburse you. Our property has a guest*

cottage, and I will make sure it's available for you and whoever might be

traveling with you.

I'm sure this is an insane request. I only hope that you know I'm

doing this because I want to show my teammates and their wives what

they mean to me. I want to give them something that will be

unforgettable, and your books have given them all so much, ummm, joy.

(You can't tell, but I'm smiling).

Please let me know at your earliest convenience.

Regards,

Alex Mills

There. That should do it, he thought. The perfect holiday gift for all of the adults. Then it hit him. Oh shit, he was going to have to meet one-on-one with this person until he unveiled the surprise. Damn.

CHAPTER FOUR

"Charlotte, I'm sorry, sweetheart," said her dance teacher, "you're just a bit too… plump to really be a ballerina, not enough elegance." Charlotte nodded, walked home, and threw away her ballet slippers.

"Charlotte, dear, perhaps your talents lie somewhere other than painting," said her art teacher. Charlotte nodded, walked home, and tossed her paints and brushes.

"Charlotte, I just don't think human resources is where your skill set lies. We're moving you to accounting," said her manager. Charlotte nodded, following the man to her new cubicle of hell.

Nothing seemed to be Charlotte's calling, nothing, until on a dare and suffering from severe sexual frustration, she wrote her first romance novel, self-publishing it. Six months later, she received a call from a publishing firm wanting her to write four more, and they were willing to pay her enough that she could quit the damn accounting job. She'd agreed, as long as she was never required to give her real name or make any appearances.

Now, ten years later, they were having the same old argument.

"Charlie, honey, you have to get out there. Your fans want to meet you, see you. If you'd just do a few book signings, then things will really pick up for you," said her publisher. Wanda DiBenedetto was a sixty-something-year-old woman with a smoker's voice and more hairspray on her body than skin.

"Wanda, we've been through this. I won't do it again. I refuse to do signings, and nothing needs to pick up. My books are selling. I'm doing just fine."

"Honey, the firm may decide to drop your books if you don't do this," she said with a hint of threat in her voice.

"If they feel that's what they have to do, then fine. I started out self-publishing. I can do it again, Wanda. I won't be manipulated into doing something I don't want to do."

"Your choice, sweetie," she said in a condescending tone. "Consider this your final warning. If you don't do at least one book signing by December 15th, they are going to pull your contract."

"I'm sorry they feel that way, considering how much money I've made them," she said quietly. "I won't be forced to step into the public again, Wanda, and you know why."

"Honey, that was years ago. No one is sending you sick letters any longer; no one is leaving underwear in the mail. It's done, over. You really need to get over it." There was silence as Charlie collected her breath, trying to calm her beating heart. "I heard from James that you two have split."

Fuck! James and his damn mouth. He was a great editor. Okay, not great, but he sucked as a lover. At least, from Charlie's minimal experience, he sucked. She'd never been very good in live relationships. The kind on paper she was fantastic with, but in person, none of her partners had been willing to put up with her quirkiness.

Spending your days writing about romance and hot, steamy sex scenes should give you an edge in the bedroom. Yet, for the two men she'd been intimate with, it was lackluster, saying she didn't have the fire her characters did. What the hell did they expect? She wasn't a character in a book. She was a real woman.

Yes, she was a woman who could stand to lose a few pounds and probably should do something with her hair, and of course, she'd never gotten around to having that eye surgery so she could rid herself of the glasses. And, yes, she was more than a little clumsy, but, oh hell, yea, she wasn't that great of a catch.

"James shouldn't open his mouth about personal things. I'm not doing this, Wanda. I refuse." She could hear the woman cursing on the other end of the line and the telltale sign of resignation.

"Fine. I'll let the board know. You're making a huge mistake, Charlotte." The use of her full name told her that Wanda was seriously pissed about this. "You won't make it without us. You won't sell one more book."

"You don't get it, Wanda. You've never understood. I don't write to sell books. I write because if I didn't, I'd explode. These books are for me, not for anyone else. If not another book sold, I wouldn't give a shit."

"Let's see how you feel in six months when you have no income," she huffed.

"Merry Christmas, Wanda." Charlie hung up the phone and looked down at her laptop. Exactly six pages written for her next book, and this time, she would need to self-publish again. She wasn't worried about it from a financial perspective. She lived in the small seaside cottage her parents left her. It was fully paid for. Her car was relatively new but also paid for, and she had a hefty savings that would see her through several years, even if she did nothing else.

Plus, what no one was aware of was the online sale of her clothing and toys inspired by the books. Tigress had been an idea born out of necessity when she couldn't find the things she needed for inspiration. Instead, she'd contacted a supplier and, via text and e-mail, set up her own store. No one knew that the website was solely owned and run by Charlie.

That was another issue her publishers had with her. She hated phone calls. If someone called her, they would immediately know CC was actually Charlotte. She preferred the anonymity of electronic communication. It was also why she controlled her fan club. She could read all the communication herself and only respond to those she felt compelled.

Over the years, she'd developed some standard communications but tried as best she could to respond to everyone.

"James," she muttered. The bastard. They'd been seeing one another for almost five years. Initially, he was charming and sweet, often bringing her flowers or planning quick weekend getaways. Then it was late nights at the office, trips out of town for business, and missed dates.

When he told Charlie he'd fallen in love with someone else, she asked

what went wrong.

"Charlotte, dear, you're a lovely girl, really. It's just in the

bedroom, you're hum-drum."

"Hum-drum?" she muttered.

Opening her fan mail inbox, she perused the messages, deleting

those she refused to answer, mostly about book signings. But it was the

most recent that caught her eye. Charlie read the e-mail three times.

A cottage in the mountains for a few weeks. She could get some

serious writing done if she took this opportunity. They wanted a book

signing, but maybe she could negotiate that. Reading the e-mail again,

she smiled.

"This guy is so sweet doing this for his friends." Her decision
made, she sent back a response.

Dear Alex,

Yes. Let's work out the details.

CC Robat

CHAPTER FIVE

Yes. Let's work out the details.

That's it? I send this guy a detailed letter pouring my heart out, and all I get back is six words? Whatever, he said yes.

Dear CC,

I'm thrilled that you've agreed to my offer. Please let me know what name to purchase an airline ticket under, departing airport, etc. I can arrange to pick you up at the airport as well. I will secure the cottage, which has Wi-Fi. I look forward to hearing from you. P.S., if it's easier to text me, this is my number...

He reread the e-mail and then hit send. Standing, he started to walk out when his phone pinged.

Thank you for the option to text – it's what I prefer. No need to send a ticket. We can work that out later. I will arrive this Tuesday evening – please send the address.

Wow! So fast. Okay then. He quickly texted the address and that he would wait in the restaurant for him if he would text an arrival time. Feeling lighter than he had in years, Ace took off toward the restaurant, seeing his teammates and their families decorating the huge tree that had become a tradition for the Steel Patriots.

"Hey! There he is," said Darby. "Calla was hoping you could help her with something she's working on for Christmas." Ace looked at the little girl and nodded. Somehow, this tiny human knew that Ace was not comfortable with touch. Although she typically flew into the waiting arms of anyone who was her target, with Ace, she always walked with slow, careful steps.

"Hi, Uncle Ace," she said, smiling at him.

"Hi, sweet Calla," he said, grinning back. "What can I help you with?" She looked over her shoulder and then toward an empty table in the corner, wiggling her finger for him to follow her. Ace grinned and obediently did as he was asked, sitting in the seat next to her.

"I'm making a present for everyone," she said quietly. "I took all these pictures with my tablet, and I want to make them into a movie. I saw a video on this kid's site that said it was easy, but it's not easy if you're only five." Ace nodded, trying to control his laughter.

"I see. Yea, that can be hard sometimes. So, these pictures, when did you take them?" he asked cautiously.

"Oh, I took them all the time!" she said excitedly. She pulled up her photo gallery and started flipping through the different photographs. There were photos of the team laughing, photos of couples kissing, Taco and Bullitt playing in the snow, even a few pictures of George and Mary hugging. But the photos that made Ace's heart stop were those of him.

In almost every photo, he lacked any emotion on his face at all. It was either serious, frowning, or only a small, almost imperceptible grin. He looked unhappy, and yet in his heart, he didn't feel unhappy.

"That's... that's a lot of pictures," he said, clearing his throat, "but it will work. What do you say you make sure you have all the pictures you want, put the ones you want to use in a folder, and then we'll sit down and make your movie?"

"Yes!" she cried triumphantly with a little fist in the air. "Thank you, Uncle Ace. Can I kiss your cheek?"

"Sure," he said, smiling. He leaned forward, and without touching his body, she gently lay her lips on his cheek, then whispered in his ear.

"I love you, Uncle Ace." Ace felt the lump rising in his throat and shoved it back down. Damn kid.

Feeling his phone vibrate once more, he looked at the text message from CC Robat and grinned.

Just so you know, I don't do well with lots of people. I hope we can work together on that.

"Preaching to the choir."

CHAPTER SIX

Charlie watched as the GPS directed her toward the small Virginia town nestled near the mountains. Snow was lightly falling, the sure signs of higher altitude and December. When she'd packed her bags for three weeks in the mountains, she quickly realized she was woefully short on appropriate clothing.

Forcing herself to make a trip to the mall first, she'd charged in, grabbed five pairs of leggings, all black and in the same size; she then grabbed five pairs of jeans after discovering the first pair fit perfectly. She then found three styles of sweaters that she felt flattered her body and bought all three, in three different colors. Next, she hit up the shoe department and bought a pair of winter boots, a pair of tall riding boots, and a new pair of running shoes.

Feeling as though she were on a roll, she whipped into the salon for a quick trim and color touch-up, then went home to pack up her life. Two huge rolling bags later, she was on her way.

Winding her way up the mountain road, the closer she got, the more she started to lose her nerve.

"What are you doing, Charlie?" she said to herself. "This person is a stranger. He could be a murderer. No, don't be ridiculous. It's a public place. Great, now you're talking to yourself." Seeing the huge red barn, she smiled with relief as she took note of all the cars in the parking lot.

Leaving her suitcases in the trunk, she grabbed her laptop and notes, thinking if he weren't there, she could work on her next project. Juggling the items in her arms, she flung her purse over her shoulder and then struggled to open the big doors. Stepping inside, her glasses fogged from the sudden heat of the room and slipped. As she went to push them up, she lost her grip on everything.

"Oh damn," she muttered, feeling her face flush with heat. Kneeling, she started to gather her things and then heard the sound of a voice that sent chills through her body.

"Here, let me help you."

CHAPTER SEVEN

Alex tried to wait patiently for CC Robat, but his patience was starting to wear thin. He'd said he would arrive at six-thirty, and it was now after seven. He looked around the restaurant seeing mostly regulars. Amanda was behind the bar, busy with holiday patrons.

He'd convinced the team to head into town and see *It's A Wonderful Life* together at the old theater, even splurging for tickets. George and Mary were watching the children, so now all he had to do was make sure no one saw CC Robat, although no one knew what he looked like.

The door opened to a woman, bundled like Nanuk of the north, and she stepped inside and then promptly dropped everything in her arms, including a very expensive laptop. Ace jumped from his seat to help her.

"Here, let me help you," he said, gathering the things up.

"I'm so sorry. I'm such a klutz," she said under her breath.

"It's no problem." He grinned at the woman, letting the sound of her soothing voice filter over his body. She had beautiful auburn hair, but that was about all Ace could see at this point.

"Wow, this place is really busy." She searched the room for a free table or for any sign of her contact moving towards her.

"Yea, lots of holiday shoppers out tonight. I'm sitting over here. Why don't you join me?" he said. What the hell am I doing? I never want to sit with strangers.

"I don't want to bother you," she said, following him to the table.

"It's no bother, I promise." In fact, he had pretty much decided that CC Robat stood him up. He would send a carefully worded message later, but for now, maybe he'd try getting to know the clumsy woman in front of him. Maybe Christmas miracles do occur.

Setting her things on the chair next to her, Charlie unbuttoned the big coat and then lay it over the back of the chair, removing her scarf and hat as well. With her glasses finally clear, she looked at the man standing beside her and felt a warm tingling deep within her belly.

He was handsome, beyond handsome. He was sexy! Black hair with startling blue eyes, lashes a woman would kill for, a full pouty mouth surrounded by a five-o-clock shadow. He was tall, but not overly, fine muscles rippling on his forearms.

"Are... are you sure you want me to join you..."

"Ace, my name is Ace."

"Ace, I'm Charlie," she said. "Charlotte, but everyone calls me Charlie."

"Nice to meet you, Charlie. What brings you way up here this time of night? We don't get a lot of strangers unless they're skiing."

"No, not skiing," she said, nibbling her bottom lip. Charlie didn't want to tell him everything in case he asked too many questions. "Just up here to work in some peace and quiet." Ace nodded his head and smiled again.

"I can understand that," he said. "I prefer quiet spaces usually myself. I'm just out here waiting for a business associate, but it doesn't look like he's going to show. Why don't we order some dinner?" he suggested.

"Are you sure?" she said. Ace nodded, calling over Amanda, who took their order and returned a few minutes later with the food. Ace kept the conversation casual and then, realizing that they'd been talking for more than two hours, decided he needed to text CC Robat.

Looks like you're delayed. Let me know when we can expect you.

Charlie looked at her phone and frowned.

Not late, been waiting here for 2 hours for u

Ace looked around the room and then noticed that Charlie was doing the same as if searching for someone. No. No, this couldn't be.

"CC Robat?" he asked. Charlie's eyes went wide, and she swallowed, nodding.

"Alex Mills?"

"Yea," he laughed. "Sorry about that. I thought you were a man."

"I thought your name was Ace," she grinned.

"My call name, road name is Ace, but Alex Mills is my real name. CC Robat?"

"Oh, yea, it's my pen name. My real name is a sort of a mix of the letters — Charlotte Christina Tabor. I reversed the letters in the last name. Everyone knows me professionally as CC Robat. Personally, it's pretty much Charlotte."

"Do you want me to call you Charlotte?" he asked, grinning at her.

"Oh no, Charlie is good. What about you? Ace or Alex?"

"Alex. I think I like when you call me Alex." Ace felt his heart skip a beat and then realized Charlie was a beautiful woman. Her hazel eyes were flecked with yellow and green, her lush, full lips a rosy red. Her skin was unmarked, with just a trace of a laugh line around her eyes. Her thick auburn hair hung straight past her shoulders.

But it was her lush curves that had Ace's body reacting. She wasn't tall, but that nipped waist beneath full breasts was making him have thoughts he wasn't used to. Then it hit him. This woman was CC Robat. This woman wrote all those steamy, sexy, hot as fuck scenes. Shit!

"So, ah, Alex, ummm, have you, I mean, did you... read my books?" Her face was crimson, and Alex thought it was cute as fuck.

"Yea," he smiled. "Everyone here was talking about them like I said in my letter. I figured I should see what all the fuss was about."

"And... and what did you think?" she asked shyly.

"I thought the writing was well done; the plots were easy to follow, and the sex was hotter than July in Amarillo." She nodded, biting her lip.

"But none of that compares to the writer."

CHAPTER EIGHT

Charlie swallowed, looking up at Alex. God, this can't be happening. First of all, he looks to be at least eight to ten years younger than her. Then, of course, there's the fact that he's freaking gorgeous! He has a body to die for and those eyes, damn those eyes.

"So, Alex, how old are you?" she asked nervously.

"How old am I?" he laughed. "Are you worried that your books may have corrupted me? I promise I'm older than I look, Charlie. I'm thirty-four, almost thirty-five. Now, fair is fair. How old are you?"

"Oh, thirty-seven," she said shyly.

"I see. I offered for you to bring family, a significant other. Since you arrived alone, I have to assume that you're not married?" She shook her head.

"No, not married, no children, no boyfriend, no girlfriend." Wincing, she looked up apologetically. "Sorry. I just recently broke up with someone I'd been dating for five years."

"I imagine he's an idiot then," said Alex nonchalantly. Charlie chuckled under her breath and nodded. "In your communication, you said you don't like being around a lot of people. I totally understand. I

don't either. In fact, just so you don't think you've done anything wrong, I

want you to know a few things about me. I'm not very comfortable with

touch. It's nothing you or anyone has done. I just struggle with human

contact."

"R-really," she whispered. "I don't think I've ever met anyone like

me." That made Alex come to attention, raising his eyebrows.

"You don't like touch? But your books…"

"They're not exactly from experience," she said, laughing

sheepishly. "It's imagination and research and… wishful thinking, I

suppose. I had a stalker early in my career. When I first started writing,

my publishers forced me to do these book tours. They're brutally

exhausting. A different city every day for days on end. This guy, I was

writing under my own name then, he… he found me and kidnapped me

from my hotel. He held me inside a small…" she swallowed, looking away

from Alex.

"You don't have to tell me, Charlie."

"It's okay. I don't know what made me be so open with you.

Usually, I'm not. He held me in this small box with air holes. I can't stand to be closed in, to have people tight around me." Alex nodded again and smiled at her.

"My experience is from childhood," he said quietly. "I was... I was kept in a cage in a closet. My foster parents let people come and touch me, poke at me like an animal in a zoo."

"Oh God, Alex," she said, reaching for his hand and then stopping, her palm hovering above his tattooed hand. The image of an eagle flying, staring back at her. Alex looked down at her hand, placing his other palm on top of hers, gently forcing it down over his own. He took a deep breath but not from the usual panic that bubbled to the surface. All he felt was warmth.

"I've been working on it," he said, staring at their hands. "My teammates, their wives, all of them are more than understanding with me. One of them, Gunner and Darby, have a little girl, Calla. She's five and the cutest darn thing. She seems to know somehow, and honestly, it's helped me so much."

"So, this? My hand on yours, it's painful?" she asked. Alex shook his head.

"No, I mean normally, yes, but for some reason... I don't know. I'm not having any issues with this for some reason." Charlie nodded.

"Well, it's getting late. Do I still have a place to stay?" she smiled. Alex laughed and stood, grabbing her laptop and notebooks.

"Definitely."

CHAPTER NINE

Alex rolled her heavy suitcases along the cleared path toward the cottage. The main houses were all behind the barn and fencing, but the cottage was toward the front of the property, far enough back from the main road that it was hidden but still secure on Patriots' property.

Charlie was walking slowly behind him, her arms still full of her laptop and purse. She'd shocked the hell out of him. First by being a woman, and second by being fucking hot as hell.

Waiting for CC Robat, Alex had this image of some professor-type in his head or an older woman who left young men in her wake. Instead, he got Charlie. Fresh-faced, innocent, shy, and the most unworldly woman he'd ever met.

"The cottage is away from everyone, so no one should bother you. We all live on-property, but we pretty much keep to ourselves. I've told everyone that you're a friend of someone I knew in the Navy. They'll know that you're here but won't bother you."

"Okay, what about meals?" she asked.

"You can come to the barn and eat or send me a text, and I'll have it brought to the cottage. There's also a full kitchen, so if you prefer to make your own meals, there are some things in there. I stocked the fridge

with some basics, but if there's anything else you need, I can always run

into town tomorrow."

Charlie looked up to see the small cottage, its light blue shutters

and snow-covered window boxes evoking charming images. Smoke

billowed from the chimney, a fire already lit inside. The soft, overstuffed

furniture was in a pale floral chintz, white and blue vases decorating the

mantel. A small Christmas tree was in the corner, covered in white lights

and blue and silver balls.

"I wasn't sure if a family was coming, so I put the tree up. I can

take it down if it bothers you," he said.

"No, no, it's lovely, really, Alex," she said, smiling. "I can see

myself getting a lot of writing done here while I'm on the property. I do

like to jog or walk. Is there a running trail?"

"Yea?" he smiled. "I love to run, and yes, we clear the trail every

day. I get up early, but if you tell me what time you want to go out, I'll

wait for you."

"Oh, no, I wouldn't want to disrupt your routine. Besides, I'm a

jogger. You look like a runner," she said, smiling. Alex felt his cheeks flush as she looked at his body. Something about that gaze made his cock twitch, and he knew he was already in dangerous territory.

"It's no bother at all. Besides, there could be wild animals. Bears should be hibernating, but you never know." Charlie's eyes flew wide, and she nodded.

"Okay, I can text you tomorrow. Probably around eight if that works for you." Alex nodded as he set the bags in the bedroom and then came back out to see her free of her winter coat, that deliciously curvy body screaming at him from across the room.

"Well, I suppose I should let you get your rest. I'll see you tomorrow, but if you need anything at all, just text me."

"Yea, yea, sure, no problem," she said nervously, following him to the door. As he reached for the handle, he turned, slamming straight into her. Instinctively, Alex reached for her shoulders, steadying her as she pushed up her cute little tortoiseshell glasses.

"Sorry," he said, still gripping her shoulders. He gently released her, and she looked disappointed. Placing his hands back on her shoulders, they both let out a sigh. "I was just going to ask you something."

"Sure, sure, anything," she said, biting her lip.

"I just wondered... of all the scenes... all the books you wrote, which is your favorite?" Charlie gave a tentative smile, nodding.

"Wow, that's tough. It's like asking which of your children are cuter," she laughed. "I like them all. I really do. But if I had to choose Rose and Thomas." He nodded thoughtfully.

"Rose and Thomas... me too," he said, smiling at her. "Goodnight, Charlie."

"Goodnight, Alex."

CHAPTER TEN

Alex practically whistled all the way back to his room, at one point nearly skipping down the walkway. Holy shit! CC Robat was a beautiful, sexy woman. More than that, she was a woman that Alex could not only tolerate for a long period of time but seemed comfortable being around. So far, they'd touched one another several times, and he'd tolerated it better than any other time in his life.

He took the steps two at a time to his suite, closing the door and pulling out the book on his nightstand about Rose and Thomas. Rose, a shy rich girl with no experience whatsoever, decided to take an adventure and experience what the world outside had to offer when she'd met Thomas, a worldly entrepreneur who offered to teach her about sex.

Their sexual experiences were off the charts hot, ranging from bondage to the use of food to enhance their experience. Alex felt his dick harden as he picked up the book, rereading the scene in front of the fireplace. Sweet little Rose chose to use one of the many dildos provided by Thomas, entertaining him with her desires and newly learned skills.

Thomas, of course, coached her through it all, telling her exactly what he wanted. Instructing her to part her sweet folds, slide her own finger in, and lick her juices. Then he told her to put that beautiful thick dildo inside.

"Fuck," moaned Alex as his dick pushed against his boxer briefs. Shoving them to his ankles, he gripped his cock and started to stroke himself, reading as he did.

"Tell me what to do, Thomas," she said breathlessly.

"You're doing so well, my beautiful Rose. Are you feeling full with that dildo? Does your wet pussy feel as though it might explode... break apart?"

"Yes, yes, Thomas. Please touch me," she begged. He reached out, gliding his long, slender fingers down the creamy flesh of her thighs, the wetness dripping out of her tightly packed hole.

"Oh, you're so ready, aren't you, Rose?"

"Y-Yes," she moaned.

"Turn it on. That's it, now in and out, my love, in and out," he directed her. He continued to touch her fleshy thighs, his cock pressing against his trousers.

"I want to see you touch yourself, Thomas." Fire filled his eyes, and he quickly lowered his pants, his huge cock springing forward for her to see for the very first time. "Oh…" she gasped.

"Touch it," he said. "Feel how hard it is, how hot it is for you, sweet Rose." She reached out with her free hand, her breasts bouncing with the movement. Thomas groaned at the touch of her fingertips. He gripped his thick cock, stroking it as she plunged the big vibrator in and out.

"I'm going to come, Thomas," she cried.

"Yes, come for me, precious girl, and take mine." He pointed his big cock at her belly, hot cum squirting on her stomach. She was the picture of eroticism; his juices spread on her body. Taking a finger, he scooped up a long strand and placed it on her lips, watching her lick it off.

"That's how it's done, sweet Rose."

"Fuck," mumbled Alex as his own hot cum streamed from his body, all over his abdomen. The chirp of his phone shook him alert. Picking it up, he smiled.

"Perfect timing."

Goodnight Alex thank you again for a lovely evening.

CHAPTER ELEVEN

Charlie watched out the window as Alex made his way back toward the big red barn. He was completely unexpected, and she worried if she would be able to follow through on helping him with his surprise.

"You're here, Charlie. Just do it."

Charlie went to work unpacking her suitcases and getting her toiletries laid out in the bathroom. The huge clawfoot tub was a nice surprise, and she definitely made a mental note to use that while she was here. Unfortunately, she also took a mental note to dream about Alex in that tub with her, water splashing over the sides, their bodies covered in the suds of bubbles.

"Don't go there, Charlie." Great, now you're talking to yourself. Finally, able to get everything placed where she wanted it, Charlie set about setting up her laptop and getting connected to the Wi-Fi. It was nearly midnight by the time she'd finally showered and got herself ready for bed.

It was funny hearing him say his favorite story was about Rose and Thomas. It always held a special meaning to her. Maybe she was hoping someone would show her the things Thomas showed Rose. At thirty-seven, Charlie should have far more experience in the arena of sex. But alas, she did not.

She'd never been the girl that people noticed when she walked into the room. Wearing glasses since the age of eleven, she was the awkward, shy girl who could barely speak around men until college. Even then, she wasn't much better, barely able to utter a few syllables here and there.

When it seemed that every occupation she tried wasn't her forte, she'd nearly given up. At one time, she even contemplated entering a convent. Unfortunately for Charlie, her thoughts of sex were more than a little overwhelming. She would often find herself thinking of sex during the most inopportune moments, like at work.

Mentioning to her one friend at the time that she couldn't clear her thoughts, Evelyn suggested she write. Of course, she'd meant for Charlie to write in a diary, not write a book. But it seemed once she started, the words just flowed, her thoughts just flowed. That first book she edited herself, chose a cover from a public image and put it out there through a self-publishing tool.

At the end of the first month, she had a nearly six-thousand-dollar check in her account. It was twice that the next month. Scrambling, she wrote another in record time, this time charging more for the book. While writing the third book, her publishers had called. Flattered and finally feeling as though she'd found her path, she agreed to meet with them.

In the room overlooking Thirty-Fourth Street, she felt overwhelmed and outmanned by the bombardment of demands and requests. But if she took the chance, she would be a published author. She signed a two-year agreement and learned a lot of lessons during that time. Spending much of her free time reading about contractual law and publishing rights, on the second contract, she was more prepared and able to refuse the book signings.

But it was still all a mistake. She should have never agreed to allow them to take over her writing, her timelines. They were brutal, and the fights over appearances after her stalker often sent Charlie into hiding for weeks on end. James tried to smooth things over since he was an editor and worked for the publisher. But even he couldn't force her to do certain things.

Now, here she was with a sexy, brilliant man only steps away, and she was frozen to her seat, again finding it easier to put the words down in text than to bring them to action.

Standing, she started the tea kettle, nibbling on her bottom lip. She opened the cabinet and grinned. Alex selected six different types of tea, and four of the six were her standards. Placing the chamomile in her cup, she waited for the water to boil.

Maybe all of this was a sign, a message for her to step out and try again. James was a mistake, and if she were being honest, although he'd said she was hum-drum in the bedroom, he was flat out boring. Lying on his back most nights with his hand wrapped around his dick, waiting for her to take a seat and ride him.

Some nights she waited, half-expecting him to pull out his phone and check his e-mail while they were going at it. The truth was, James just didn't excite her. Her body reacted, sure, but he didn't inspire her to do things or write things. Not the way Alex had in only a few short hours.

Her head was spilling with new ideas and plot twists. The thought of his hands roaming over her body, touching her in places she could only dream about. She thought of the tattooed, veiny hands gripping her breasts, gliding down her skin to find their way to her deep, wet folds.

Moaning, Charlie leaned back on the sofa, her hands gliding beneath the waistband of her pajamas. She was so wet as she touched herself. She was already jerking toward an orgasm. Painting the face of Alex above her, she rubbed, squeezing one breast tightly.

"Oh, Alex," she moaned. As the tea kettle whistled, so did Charlie's body, shaking with pleasure. Rising, she poured the tea and smiled. Reaching for her phone, she sent one final text goodnight and then tucked herself beneath the covers, dreaming of blue eyes and dark knights.

CHAPTER TWELVE

"Morning," said Alex, smiling at his teammates as he grabbed a slice of bacon off the pile on the plate. He was dressed in his running attire, a fleece jacket pulled over his head, his running gloves and hat shoved in his pocket. Ghost looked up at him and then over at Whiskey and Zulu.

"You're chipper this morning. Your friend get into town?" asked Gunner.

"Yea, yea," he said, nodding with a smile.

"Oh fuck, it's a woman, isn't it?" said Whiskey, smiling at their friend.

"What? No, no, it's not. Yea, it's a woman," he said, barely able to contain himself. He didn't want to tell the guys who the woman was, but he also had never kept a secret from his teammates. Alex looked around the room.

"The girls have gone into town for early shopping," said Doc. "What's the deal, Ace? I mean, we could give a fuck if you bring a woman to the cottage, but... you?"

"Well, I wanted to give you all something for Christmas, something that has affected all of you, all of us," said Alex.

"And this person is the gift?" said Hawk. Ace nodded.

"It's CC Robat."

"CC… what the fuck? So, it's a woman. I mean, she's a woman… the author?" said Ghost.

"Yea, a beautiful, curvy, fucking angel-faced woman," he said, smiling.

"Oh. My. God. You like this woman," said Zulu. Ace frowned and nodded, his fingers twisting with one another. "Brother, don't be embarrassed. This is fucking awesome."

"I wanted her to do a book signing at the Page Turner, but she's like me. She doesn't like crowds. After a signing early in her career, she was kidnapped and held in a tiny box with air holes."

"Fuck," growled Ghost.

"Yes, she just gets really nervous, so if you see us together, don't crowd, and for God's sake, don't tell the girls who she is. Her real name is

Charlotte, but she goes by Charlie, so just call her that." They all nodded, grinning at the younger man.

"You know it will all work out, right, brother?" said Tango.

"Easy for all of you to say. You have women in your lives, or if you don't, you know you could get one at a moment's notice. I can't... I mean... I can... I..." He stared off, and Hawk sat next to him.

"Listen, Ace. I know I'm an asshole when it comes to women sometimes, but believe me, if this woman is for you, you'll know it, and everything will work out."

"Are you going running?" asked Whiskey.

"Yea, she wanted to jog the trails this morning, so..." A noise behind them had them all turning to see George with a pretty auburn-haired woman, her body encased in running tights and a sweatshirt, carrying her laptop.

"Charlie!" he said, standing. "Charlie, come in. Come in."

"Found this little lady out there searchin' for you. Seems upset by something, and you boys know how I feel about an upset woman. Ain't happenin' round me."

"What's wrong, honey?" asked Zulu. Charlie immediately took a step back, and Zulu raised his hands. "I'm not going to hurt you, honey. I'm a friend of Alex."

"They're all my friends, Charlie. Every man in this room is my friend. No one would harm you." She nodded and then handed him her laptop. "Something broken?"

"N-no, it's him. H-he's back."

"Who?" said Ghost, standing quickly, causing Charlie to jump again.

"You guys really have to learn to do that shit quieter," said Ace, glaring at them. George, without even touching Charlie, waved her into the big kitchen.

"Let me get you some tea, honey. You hungry?" She nodded, smiling at the man. Ace took the laptop and stared at the message on her fan board.

"This one?" he asked as she nodded her head. *We never finished our lesson.* The men in the room shuffled and stood behind Ace, reading the message as if they could see something that neither of them was able to.

"What does it mean?" asked Doc.

"I... I was kidnapped... at a b-book signing early in my career. The m-man," she shivered and shook her head. That's when the entire room held their breath as Ace reached for her hand, linking it with his own. She looked down and let out a long slow breath, Ace smiling up at her. "H-he said he wanted to teach me some lessons f-for my books. I was held in a b-box... a small..." her breathing started picking up, and Doc rushed to kneel beside her.

"Breathe, honey. Slow, in and out. That's it, just look at Alex." Somehow, Doc knew that the man beside her would help to calm her nerves. "Take a drink... slow... better?" She nodded.

"H-he's coming for m-me again," she said, letting the tears slide down her cheeks.

"No, he's not," said Alex, squeezing her fingers. "This property is secure, and you are protected. I will protect you. We're going to move you from the cottage to the suites here in the barn. I'll make sure that no one gets to you."

"F-for how long," she said with tear-filled eyes. "I can't stay here forever."

"Let's talk about that later, okay? For now, we'll go get your bags and bring you back here. We have plenty of space, and you'll be closer to all of us. This man doesn't have a clue where you are right now. Did you tell anyone where you were going?"

"No, no one." Ace nodded.

"Let me just introduce you to everyone, so you know who is who." She nodded.

"George and Mary live upstairs, as do Razor and Isabella. Those are the only couples living here. The other single guys in the barn are Hawk, Eagle, Skull, Ice, Axe, and Blade. Oh, and me," he said, grinning.

"The other guys you see here are all married. Ghost is my team lead, and he's married to Grace. They have a little boy JT and another on the way. Doc is married to Bree, and they have one on the way as well, as does Whiskey and Kat."

"So, don't drink the water?" she said in an attempt to lighten the mood. The others all chuckled, nodding at the woman.

"Then we have Zulu and Gabrielle, or we call her Angel eyes. They have twin boys, Wade and Tyler. That's Tango. He's married to Taylor, and they're expecting as well. Gunner is married to Darby, the woman I told you who owns the bookstore."

Charlie stiffened and started to stand, but Alex held her close, not allowing her to leave.

"We're not going to make you do anything you don't want to do, honey. You have my word." She nodded. "Lastly is Razor and Isabella. That's it."

"I-I'll never be able to remember all that," she said quietly.

"No need, Charlie," said Ghost. "Just know that any of these faces, and the faces of our wives whom I'm sure you'll meet, are friendly faces. We're not going to ruin Alex's surprise by saying who you really are, just that you're a friend."

"Oh, geez, you all read the books?" she said, flushing a bright pink. Ghost smiled at the woman and unfolded his arms.

"If I didn't think you'd run for the hills, I'd hug you, honey. I have a great marriage, but I can tell you that my life in the bedroom got much better with us sharing those books."

"Same," said Whiskey. "I know you're a lot like Ace and don't care for touch, but believe me, I'd love to give you a hug as well. I think what I'm curious about, though, is you write these books about…"

"Sex?" Whiskey nodded. "Sex with confident women." He nodded again, along with ten other heads. "And you're all wondering how someone so meek, shy, and seemingly afraid of her own shadow could write those books?"

"It does seem odd," said Doc, giving her a sly grin.

"I know. I wrote the first one just needing to get everything that was in my head out! Then it was the second, and then the third. My ideas kept coming, and I didn't even know from where. I didn't know how to control it. I mean, I was doing a lot of research on the internet and reading other authors getting inspiration. When the abduction happened, under my real name, I started writing under a pseudonym. After that, I made sure I had control over everything from the fan page to my media appearances which were zero."

"Your publisher okay with that?" asked Razor.

"No, not at all. In fact, we had a big argument before I left to come here. They said if I didn't do a book signing before December 15th, they would drop me as an author."

"Damn, can they do that?" asked Zulu.

"It's in the contract, and I've been holding them off for years now. I just can't, though. I just… if someone sees me… I… my life is over with. I love writing, but I love the anonymity of it. I don't want every pervert or creep out there to think because I write the books, I live it. I just can't do an appearance…"

"It's okay. You won't have to," said Ace. "We won't ask you to do anything you're not comfortable with. For now, let's get your bags and come back here. When we're done, you and I will take our run, and then we can chat about what to do next."

"I-I'm sorry to bring this to your door," she said to the group.

"Honey, there is nothing to be sorry about," said Ghost. "Anyone who can make Alex smile like that is welcome here for as long as they like."

CHAPTER THIRTEEN

"Wow, this is nice," she said, stepping into the suite next to Ace's. "It's like an upscale hotel suite. Are all the rooms like this?"

"Mary and George are expanding theirs, basically combining two suites so that they have more like a small apartment. Most of my teammates have built homes on the property. Razor and Bella are building now." She nodded, looking at the familiar chintz love seat, the same pattern as the sofa in the cottage.

"You didn't want to build a house?" she asked.

"Never really saw a need." He wanted to say 'until now' but didn't want to freak her out. "I'm close to the computer room here, and if the guys are working a job, I stick close to the computers and communication room. Eventually, if I were to meet someone, then yes, I would want to build." Nodding, she smiled at him.

"Well, I can unpack all this later. I need to get some fresh air and clear my head." Alex smiled at her, opening the suite doors once again. Down the back stairs, they stepped out onto the porch, facing the various path options and the huge overlook of the valley.

"Wow, this is beautiful," she said quietly.

"Yea, it is. All this land belonged to Ghost's father. When he died, he left the land, the shop, and the barn to him. When the guys all retired, they decided to start the motorcycle club. We all ride and love our motorcycles. Razor, Skull, and Tango are the real geniuses behind building the custom bikes, which is our number one income maker, next to the restaurant and bar."

"I remember you saying that in your letter. It was part of why I decided to come. It sounds intriguing." Alex felt a twist in his gut and looked up at her.

"Charlie? You know that you can't write about anything you hear from us, right? No old missions, nothing of our time in the military."

"Oh, yes, I'm sorry if I gave you that impression. I would never do that, ever. I'm big on privacy, and obviously, I wouldn't violate someone else's."

"Thank you," he said, smiling. Reaching out his hand, she looked down at his gloved hand and let her mitten-covered hand slide into his. "Ready?" Nodding, they took off in a casual walk, Alex telling her about specific parts of the trail, pointing out the outer buildings on the property.

He took the trail winding behind the shop and the clinic and then headed toward the outlook of the valley.

The temperatures were cold but not bitterly so. Each breath came out in a frosty fog, the sharp chill hitting their faces as they moved. Stopping at the bench where Ghost's father proposed to his mother, they looked out over the snow-covered valley, Christmas lights twinkling in the distance.

"It's so beautiful up here," she said, looking off to the distance. "You know, I would never use anything you all tell me in my books or even your names, but this... this view, this scenery? I will definitely use that in my books. It's unbelievably romantic and picturesque here."

"Is it?" smiled Ace, tilting his head toward her.

"It is," she blushed. "I mean, I can picture my characters in this exact spot, just like this, talking and..." She stopped, blushing, and Ace wanted to reach out and beg for her to continue.

"Tell me, what would happen to these romantic characters of yours?" he pleaded. The wind blew across the landscape, her auburn hair flying into her face. Charlie swallowed and looked up into the younger man's handsome face.

"He... he would reach out and brush the hair from her face, gently tucking it behind her ear," she whispered. Alex removed his glove, his warm fingers brushing the strands of hair from her face, securing it behind one delicate ear. He allowed his fingers to linger there for a moment and then gently followed the curve of her ear, his fingers massing her small lobe. His skin touching her own, he was prepared for a reaction in his body, but definitely not the one he got. Sizzles of electricity coursed through him at the touch of her skin; his fingers almost singed from the contact.

"What next?" he said in a deep voice.

"I... I think... h-he would lay his palm against her cheek, feeling her skin." Doing as she described, Alex let his palm cup her cheek, the heat from her flush seeping into his hand, his callused thumb rubbing gently over her cheekbone. "Then... then he would take a step forward... close, but not too close."

He smiled, nodding at her as he took a step toward her, their toes now touching.

"I... I'm not sure..."

"I think I have it from here," he said, grinning at her. Lowering his head, his mouth hovered above hers as he watched her face for any signs of panic, waiting for his own body to feel the panic that typically came. He didn't touch her other than his hand still laying against her cheek, didn't press for more than just this. Then, gently, he lowered his lips to hers, just resting them there. When Charlie let out a long hot breath against his mouth, he opened as she slid her tongue between his lips.

Their mouths gently nibbled, tasting one another, his hand still cupping her soft, smooth cheek as their tongues melded together. The taste of her filled his senses, the feeling of her plush, soft lips against his own. Reluctantly, Alex pulled back, taking a step backward.

"I'm sorry if that was…"

"No," she gasped for air, "no, it was… perfect. I… you… you didn't seem to have any trouble with that," she grinned. Charlie touched her lips, letting a nervous giggle escaped her lips.

"It was pretty perfect, and no, I didn't have any issues whatsoever," Alex agreed.

"I've obviously been kissed before, but wow, Alex, that was... that was really special," she said breathlessly. Leaning forward, he kissed her forehead and grinned.

"Couldn't agree more, honey. That's the first time I've ever made the first move, willingly made the move, and not freaked out from it. I don't know what this is, Charlie, but I've felt connected to you since you walked in that door of the restaurant. I'm not willing to let that go yet. I hope you won't either." She could only nod at him, too stunned to say anything else. "Come on, let's finish our walk and get warm. The guys are going to want to chat about tracking this fan down."

"You had to bring that up, huh?"

"Can't let anyone touch you, Charlie. No one except me, anyway." Alex grinned as he started to walk down the trail, turning to see a shocked look on Charlie's face. He held his hand to her waiting until she lay her fingers gently in his palm.

This trip was definitely turning out to be more than Charlie had bargained for. Alex Mills might be hesitant to touch a woman, but when he did... wowza!

CHAPTER FOURTEEN

"So, Charlie, can you explain the details of your kidnapping? I know it will be difficult, hun, but it would be really helpful," said Ghost.

Charlie nodded, looking at the room full of men. Normally, she would be feeling a bit of panic with this many people, especially men in such close proximity, but she found that she was not having her normal hyperventilation or heart palpitations. One reason was that they left the conference room door open. The other more obvious reason was Alex sitting beside her, his fingers resting against her own.

"Sure, it was the first year that I signed with my publisher. Before that, I was self-published, and if I'm being honest, I should have stuck to that."

"Why do you say that, Charlie?" asked Zulu.

"Well, when you sign with a publisher, particularly someone like me who was a new, unheard of author, you often sort of sell your soul. They control everything, even sometimes the content. I would write what I typically did, and they would ask me to change characters or locations or even details. At one point, they wanted me to use ghostwriters, and I refused." Zulu nodded for her to continue.

"Anyway, my original contract had that I was to do twenty book signing events a year."

"That seems like a lot," said Whiskey. Charlie nodded.

"It is. When you consider that they wanted me to put out at least two books a year, that's a tremendous number of events."

"Wait? Two a year? By that count, you should have over twenty books to your name. I... we've only seen fifteen," said Tango.

"That's right, because the first four were written under my real name, Charlotte C. Tabor. When the incident happened, I refused to use my real name again. Anyway, I was trying to finish a book, and they sent me out on a tour for the last one. I was getting all these strange notes, flowers, and things at my hotel room doors in every city. Originally, I just thought it was some fan, but when the notes started to have details..."

"It's okay, honey," said Alex, rubbing his fingers over her own. "You don't have to tell us anything you don't want to."

"I think you need to know. The notes gave a lot of detail about things he wanted to... to do to me. Most of it followed familiar lines from my books. If I had written about bondage, it was him taking it to the next level with torture. Or if it was about..." She sucked in a breath and looked away, brushing a tear from her cheek.

"Charlie, you don't have to tell us all the details, honey," said Ghost. "Did you keep copies?" She shook her head.

"N-no. The publisher said they would take care of everything."

"Did they?" asked Razor.

"Not hardly," she scoffed. "I asked them to keep it quiet, hire security, and maybe a private investigator. Instead, they contacted the police and the media. It was a nightmare. The press wouldn't leave me alone. They knew where I was every second of the day, which meant this crazy person did too. The police said there wasn't anything they could do. I was terrified to leave my hotel room."

"But you did?" said Gunner.

"Y-yes. My... my editor, James... we later started dating, but we weren't at the time. James and Wanda from the publishing company sent me a note saying they wanted to meet me in the hotel bar. I left my room to meet them and was abducted in the elevator. H-he put a black hood over my head and... I'm not sure where we went from there. The security cameras were somehow not working. I know we drove somewhere, but I don't know where. He knocked me out and placed m-me..." She sucked

in a huge gulp of air, her hands starting to shake.

"Enough," said Ace, standing.

"N-no... it's o-okay... they need to know. When I woke up, I was in

a box... like a coffin with big air holes. Big enough for three fingers to fit

through but not my whole hand. I kept screaming, begging him to let me

out. I could hear shuffling, some whispering with another person but

nothing else. Two days later, I woke up to someone breaking down a

door, and then the police opening the box."

"Jesus, Charlie," said Doc. "Were you physically harmed?"

"A bump on my head, but that was it. I was in the hospital for a

few days and then under the care of a therapist, but I refused to go out

much after that. The publisher was angry with me. They said I was hot in

the media. That I should strike while my name was out there. I just

couldn't. I shut down."

"I got my lawyer to rewrite the contract claiming duress and a

whole bunch of other stuff. I reclaimed total control of my content, the

fan page, covers, everything."

"This guy James, the one you dated for a bit, what was his role?" asked Zulu.

"He was my editor. I really didn't think he was very good. In fact, I caught him several times rewriting complete scenes. Initially, I tried to get him removed and then, well, I had to go to New York for some meetings, and he seemed nice. He was sweet to me, understanding. It wasn't ever truly romantic, more convenient." Alex said nothing, simply staring down.

"When did you stop seeing one another?" asked Ghost.

"About eight months ago. He was cheating on me, and he said…"

"He said what?" growled Ace.

"H-he said I was hum-drum in the bedroom. Actually, threatened me in an off-handed sort of way, saying it would be a shame if my readers knew that the writer of erotic romance was terrible in the bedroom." Her face burned with embarrassment and humiliation, tears filling those gorgeous hazel eyes, and Alex wanted to kill James small dick.

"Sounds like a man with performance issues," said Hawk, winking at Charlie. She chuckled, nodding.

"You're not far off. He definitely wasn't anything to write home about. My publisher, when I called to tell her I was refusing the book signings, she actually brought his name up, saying she heard we weren't seeing one another any longer."

"Does anyone know you're here?" asked Ace.

"No, absolutely not. I live in the Outer Banks, far away from everyone. No one even knows my address. I use a P.O. Box in South Carolina as my address. I have an arrangement with the mailbox service, and he sends my mail to me at another P.O. Box in North Carolina. I don't really have any friends to speak of. No one I'm dating, and when we argued last week, I basically said I was dropping them as my publisher. I didn't leave a temporary forwarding address; I never have my location active on my phone for fear of something happening. I drove straight here non-stop."

"Who would gain by this?" asked Ghost. Charlie shrugged, shaking her head.

"I have no idea. I mean, writers, actors, performers all do things sometimes to keep their names in the spotlight. I've always wanted to stay out of the spotlight."

"That seems strange, honey. I mean, writing books like this, that are so popular, you had to know you would be in the spotlight," said Ghost.

"I know what you mean, but remember, I didn't write these to be popular or to sell books. I wrote them for me. I wrote them to get my visions out of my head and on paper. I wrote them to prove that I was a woman. A woman with real feelings and desires, even if no one else understood them."

"We definitely understood them," grinned Tango. Charlie blushed a bright pink, smiling at the big man.

"I'm glad. It makes me happy that my books allowed you and your wives to speak more openly in the bedroom. It's part of why I did it. I've always been the shy, geeky, awkward girl in the room. Tortoiseshell glasses, not tall, not short, not fat, not thin. I'm the wallpaper that no one notices. The books were a way for me to prove I was noticeable... without being noticed. Does that make sense?"

"First, you are totally noticeable. I noticed you. Second, it makes perfect sense to me, honey," said Ace. He looked at his brothers around the room. "All of us, especially Ghost's original team, what we do, what we did wasn't to be noticed or given medals or considered heroes. We did it because we loved freedom. We loved helping the underdog. We all understand why you did what you did."

"Charlie," said Ghost, "we're going to help you with this, hun, because it's what we do and because you're one of us." He looked at Ace and winked, making the man squirm in his seat.

"I-I have money. I can pay you." Ghost shook his head, raising a hand to stop her.

"Family, honey, you're family." She nodded.

"A few rules, Charlie," said Whiskey. "Don't leave the property without one of us. Let Ace do his fancy work to your phone and computer. Give him access to your fan page. He might be able to trace the e-mails from there. Don't take any unnecessary calls while you're here. Try to let things go to voicemail, and if you get something strange, come to us immediately." She nodded and stood.

"I can't thank you all enough for this, really. I've never had so many people willing to help me."

"Like we said, honey," said Zulu. "Family."

"Charlie, if you don't mind waiting in the kitchen, I'll be out in a minute," said Ace. She smiled, and then, daring to step out of her comfort zone, she leaned forward and placed a kiss on his cheek. As she exited, Charlie pulled the door closed. Ace turned to see all eyes on him, mouths open.

"I know," he said, shaking his head, "I know, and I can't explain it, but as I'm sure you're all aware, she is mine."

CHAPTER FIFTEEN

Charlie left the conference room, heading down the long hallway toward the back of the barn. She heard loud conversation and followed the sounds to see eight women sitting around the enormous kitchen table. George was stirring something in a huge pot.

"H-hello," she said shyly, stepping into the room.

"Oh, hello, Charlie," said George. "Ladies, this is a friend of Ace's. Charlie, these are the beautiful women of this sorted group of assholes, including myself in that mix."

"Hi, I'm Grace. Ace said he had a friend from the Navy ask if his sister could stay with us. Welcome!" The woman standing before Charlie was exceptionally pretty, her short auburn hair a shade closer to red than Charlie's own. She was petite with curves and had the most adorable little boy in her arms.

"And who is this cutie?" asked Charlie, dying to reach out and squeeze those fat little cheeks. He was fisting a cookie of some sort that she was sure he would scream bloody murder if anyone tried to take it away.

"This is JT, my son. I'm married to Ghost. We're expecting our second next year," she said, smiling as she rubbed her little belly.

"That's wonderful, congratulations!"

"Thank you," she smiled. "It's a bit of a surprise considering we're both mid-forties. Well, don't tell Ghost I said this, but he's on the back side of forty." She winked at Charlie, and she couldn't help but chuckle.

"Let me introduce you to everyone else. This is Mary, George's love. Kat, married to Whiskey; Bree, married to Doc; Taylor, married to Tango; Bella, married to Razor; Gabi or the guys usually call her Angel eyes, married to Zulu; Darby, married to Gunner; and Amanda is dating Ice. I think that's our mixed bag of crazy."

"Wow, I'll never be able to remember that, but you're all so uniquely beautiful," she said, blushing as she said the words.

"Okay, you can join us any time you want to!" said Bree.

"Seriously, I don't have a lot of female friends, or male. I'm kind of shy and awkward, but you guys are really a poster for what beauty variety represents."

Grace cocked her head at the woman smiling, a low hum coming from her as she thought about her statement. Shy. Not a lot of friends.

Indirectly friends with their Ace. This woman was perfect for him. She looked toward Bree and Gabi smiling. It was as if the entire table suddenly knew what to do.

"So, Charlie, you're not dating anyone?" asked Darby casually.

"N-no, I'm not very good with men," she said, blushing.

"Well, you've met Ace. What do you think of our sexy resident geek?" asked Taylor.

"Oh, oh, yes, well, he's... I mean, we're only friends. We both..." she muttered under her breath and then collected her thoughts. "He's very sexy, very nice, and a few years younger than me."

"That's a solid list you've got goin' there, Charlie, but age doesn't matter," said Kat. "Whiskey is almost twenty years older than me, and no one says a thing about it. I hate the stereotypical shit people put on age."

"Or race," piped in Gabi with a nod toward Mary and George. "I mean, look at Zulu and me, or Mary and George. We couldn't be more opposite in every single way. None of that matters if you click, sweetie."

Charlie nodded her head and frowned, looking up to see George's sympathetic face staring at her. He gave her a quick grin and a wink, telling her they all meant well.

"I-I know what you mean. Really, I do, but..."

"Listen," said Grace, "we're all reading these amazing books by CC Robat. Have you heard of them?" Charlie nearly choked on her tongue but only shook her head. "Anyway, they are phenomenal and will change your mind about sex and relationships. Why don't I lend you my copies, and you can join in on our book club conversations while you're here?"

"Oh-oh that's really nice of you, but I'll just... I'll just download them to my tablet. But, sure, I'd love to be a part of your discussion." What the hell are you doing, Charlie? Maybe this would be good research for her, find out what they like, dislike, what she should do more of in the next books.

"Awesome! In the meantime, honey, why don't you read the first one and think about how to approach Ace?" said Darby. "I mean, maybe the way Alexis works with Max will work for you and Ace."

"I appreciate it, ladies. Really, I do. I mean, I don't know Ace well, but he's sweet. He's sexy, and, oh gosh, I have no idea how he feels or what he's willing to explore," she said, fanning herself.

"Why don't you ask him?" said the deep voice behind her. Charlie closed her eyes, swallowing as she turned to look into the face of the very handsome, extraordinarily sexy Alex. "Why don't you ask him directly how he feels?"

"B-because I c-can't," she stuttered, pushing her glasses further up her nose.

"You can," he said, stepping into the room. The women all pushed against the counters closer to George, watching the scene play out like one of their books. They were all smiling, holding hands with the woman next to them.

"A-Alex... I like you... a lot. I'm older than you, and I don't know..."

"I like older women, and you're only three years older than me, not fifty," he grinned. Reaching for her waist, he lay his hand gently at the curve of her hip, slowly pulling her closer.

Grace opened her mouth, gawking at the events happening in front of them. Their Ace... their sweet, shy, awkward, contact-phobic Ace was reaching out to touch a woman voluntarily.

"Y-you don't mind?"

"No. I don't mind, and I'd like to see if we can get to know one another better. I can't promise anything, Charlie. Neither can you. But what do you say? You and me... spend the next week or so getting to know one another?"

Charlie turned to see the shocked, smiling faces behind her, all the women giving her a little nod and push with their facial expressions. She looked over their heads to see George, a big wink, and a grin.

Ace looked behind him to see his brothers all standing there, their arms folded, grinning at him. Hawk shook his head and then lifted his hands, shooing Ace closer. Finally frustrated, he couldn't stand it any longer.

"Oh, for fuck's sake, kiss the woman!" Ace growled at his friend and then turned, smiling down at Charlie.

"I already did once," he said, "but I'm sure willing to try again." Charlie could only nod as he lowered his lips to hers, standing a few inches apart, but their lips locked together. Lost in the scent of Ace, his cologne, his masculinity, she didn't dare break the contact for fear it would never come again. When the applause broke out around them, both individuals flushed a deep crimson.

"Alright, 'nuff kissin' in my kitchen," said George. "Out! Dinner is ready, and we'll be bringin' it out. Miss Charlie, you come see me if he doesn't treat you right, ya hear?"

"Yes, sir." Charlie smiled as Ace laced their fingers together, looking down at the locked hands. "All okay?" she asked. Ace sucked in a deep breath, then looked down again, prepared for the panic or need to run. Instead, he only felt warmth.

"Perfect."

CHAPTER SIXTEEN

The team watched as Charlie left the conference room, her shoulders slumped in defeat and fear, that thick mane of auburn hair swinging at her back. Their eyes turned to Ace, who was watching every movement she made. Finally turning back to the table, he bit his bottom lip and looked up.

"She's terrified. I can't blame her," he said. Ghost nodded.

"You think this is the same stalker?" asked Whiskey.

"I don't know. I haven't had a chance to dig into her electronics yet, but I can tell you that the whole ordeal with her publisher pisses me off. Seems to me this Wanda and the shrimp dick, James, might have done more for her, helped her in some way, than what they did the first time around."

Ace pulled up her fan page, connecting it to the television in the room for all to see. It had several photos of her book covers, a stock scene behind them of clouds, but noticeably missing was a photo of Charlie. He glanced at some of the comments.

"You changed my life... thank you!"

"I don't mind giving blowjobs now... my boyfriend says you're the shit!"

"Where can I buy the double-headed dildo? My girlfriend and I are going to get adventurous."

"Holy fuck," mumbled Hawk. "A double-headed dildo?"

"That's what you got out of all that!" said Gunner. "You stupid shit, look at the comments. Everyone loves her. Get into the e-mails, Ace." He nodded, giving a death stare to Hawk.

"Here, these are the ones. I don't think she knows there are three more than what she showed me. Look at the time stamps. They came in successively about eight minutes apart." Ace pulled up the first one and read.

You and I are meant to be together. I will find you, and we will complete our chapter.

You can't run from me. You will act out our final scene.

"Fuck, this guy is off his rocker," said Zulu.

"Yea, which makes him unpredictable," said Ace. "I'm going to trace the e-mail address and then put a tracker on it for any return replies. If I don't get anything in the next few days, I may respond and try to draw him out. I don't want to do that. I don't want to put her in any danger, but it might be our only way."

"What about this guy James and the woman... Wanda?" asked Tango.

"I haven't had time to pull anything on them yet, but I will. I don't like that they were there the first time around, and somehow, they're still in the picture now. Plus, the way this woman, Wanda, was bullying her to do the book signings really bugs me as well."

Ghost nodded, looking at the younger man. Although he was only about twelve years younger than Ghost, he'd always thought of him like a son or at least a younger brother, wanting to protect him. What he was realizing is that Ace didn't need anyone to protect him. He only needed people to understand him.

"You're different," said Whiskey, grinning at him.

"Different?" asked Ace.

"Yea, man, in a good way. You're more... relaxed. You're sitting nearly on top of Zulu and Tango. Usually, you would be standing or pushed over by the door. It's fucking cool, brother. If this is Charlie's

doing, keep that beautiful girl around." Ace smiled, nodding at the room.

"I can't explain it. She came into the restaurant the other night

and dropped her shit all over the floor. She was so nervous and jumpy. I

would usually just watch from afar, but I couldn't. I immediately stood up

and helped her collect her things. I had no clue who she was at that

point, but I invited her to sit with me."

Eyebrows went up around the room, and Doc gave a small smirk

to his friend across the table.

"We ate together and talked for two hours before I figured out

that she was CC Robat. It was so strange. Then this morning, we went for

a walk, and I actually held her hand and kissed her."

"Well, brother, I'd say that's an indication the woman is right for

you," smiled Ghost. "What are you going to do about it?"

Ace just stared at his hands for a minute and then looked around

the room at the faces he called family. Although he annoyed the ever-

loving-fuck out of him, he stared at Hawk, who finally spoke.

"Oh, for fuck's sake, go tell the girl, you idiot." Ace stood, walking down the hall toward the kitchen. As he approached the door, he heard Charlie's voice.

"I appreciate it, ladies. Really, I do. I mean, I don't know Ace well, but he's sweet. He's sexy, and, oh gosh, I have no idea how he feels or what he's willing to explore," she said, fanning herself.

"Why don't you ask him?" said the deep voice behind her. Charlie closed her eyes, swallowing as she turned to look into the face of the very handsome, extraordinarily sexy Alex. "Why don't you ask him... me directly how I feel?"

"B-because I c-can't," she stuttered, pushing her glasses further up her nose.

"You can," he said, stepping into the room. The women all pushed against the counters, closer to George, watching the scene play out like one of their books. They were all smiling, holding hands with the woman next to her.

"A-Alex... I like you... a lot. I'm older than you, and I don't know..."

"I like older women, and you're only three years older than me, not fifty," he grinned. Reaching for her waist, he lay his hand gently at the curve of her hip, slowly pulling her closer.

Grace opened her mouth, gawking at the events happening in front of them. Their Ace... their sweet, shy, awkward, contact-phobic Ace was reaching out to touch a woman voluntarily.

"Y-you don't mind?"

"No. I don't mind, and I'd like to see if we can get to know one another better. I can't promise anything, Charlie. Neither can you. But what do you say? You and me... spend the next week or so getting to know one another?"

Charlie turned to see the shocked, smiling faces behind her, all the women giving her a little nod and push with their facial expressions. She looked over their heads to see George, a big wink, and a grin.

Ace looked behind him to see his brothers all standing there, their arms folded, grinning at him. Hawk shook his head and then lifted his hands, shooing Ace closer. Finally frustrated, he couldn't stand it any longer.

"Oh, for fuck's sake, kiss the woman!" Ace growled at his friend and then turned, smiling down at Charlie.

"I already did once," he said, "but I'm sure willing to try again." Charlie could only nod as he lowered his lips to hers, standing a few inches apart, but their lips locked together. Lost in the scent of Ace, his cologne, his masculinity, she didn't dare break the contact for fear it would never come again. When the applause broke out around them, both individuals flushed a deep crimson.

"Alright, 'nuff kissin' in my kitchen," said George. "Out! Dinner is ready, and we'll be bringin' it out. Miss Charlie, you come see me if he doesn't treat you right, ya hear?"

"Yes, sir." Charlie smiled as Ace laced their fingers together, looking down at the locked hands. "All okay?" she asked. Ace sucked in a deep breath, then looked down again, prepared for the panic or need to run. Instead, he only felt warmth.

"Perfect."

CHAPTER SEVENTEEN

Dinner at Club Steel was loud on any night, but on a night when the entire team was present with wives and children, it was chaotically loud. Top that with the fact that the tree decorations were being completed, the kids were wanting to touch everything, and it seemed that peace and quiet would have to wait until after the New Year.

"You okay?" asked Ace.

"Yea, it's just there's so many of them," she laughed. "I like them, though, Alex. I don't say that about many people, believe me. But all of these people have made me feel welcome and important, and they don't even know me. Your team, they were so nonjudgmental and kind in that room. Then the women, when I walked into the kitchen, they just enveloped me right away."

"Yea, they're all an amazing group of people. Not one of them has ever judged me for the way I am, or maybe I should say the way I was," he grinned. "You've changed me, Charlie, and I damn sure like the changes that are happening here."

"Me too," she whispered.

"It's scary. I know it is, and I'm not sure what will happen when we decide to take it to the next level, but I know I'd like to find out." Charlie stared at him, wondering if she'd actually heard him correctly.

"Y-you want to try to be... I mean to have... like you and me in bed..." Ace couldn't help but chuckle at her stammering.

"Yes, Charlie," he said, kissing her cheek. "Is that so hard to believe? You're a beautiful, intelligent, sexy woman, and I've never felt this kind of connection to anyone before."

"I feel the same... about you, I mean," she said, pushing her glasses up again. "I've never been very comfortable with men, and yet you made me feel like I could be me right away. James, he-he hurt me when he said I was hum-drum in the bedroom. I want to be like my characters, you know. It's why I write what I do. I want to be them, but he just laid there like I was supposed to take control." She bit her lip and looked away, prompting Ace to place a finger beneath her chin, turning her to face him.

"He is a fucking moron, honey. You are beautiful, and I feel certain you will be amazing in bed." Ace squirmed a bit, trying to adjust his ever-rising dick. He didn't want to scare her, nor did he want to embarrass himself.

"I-I'd like to go upstairs now." Ace's face fell in disappointment. "With you, I want to go upstairs with you. Is that okay?"

"Yea, honey, that's okay." Ace stood and took her hand, weaving their way around the tables toward the first steel door. He could feel all eyes following them, and just when he thought they were clear, the first steel door shutting behind them, a loud roar of applause broke out. "Sorry about that. They mean well."

"It's okay," she laughed as they walked upstairs. Opening the door to her room, she nodded for him to enter and sat on the loveseat. Still holding hands, he pulled her closer, his warm lips trailing across her forehead, down her jaw, and finally to her lips.

Charlie could feel her nipples hardening and the definite feeling of wetness between her legs. Reaching out, she ran her fingers across Ace's chest.

"Is-is this okay? Do you like to be touched like this?"

"I don't know, Charlie. I mean, you're the first woman I've been able to let touch me almost immediately. Normally, I would feel overwhelmed, sort of claustrophobic, but with you, I don't. If we get to this point, usually, I ask the woman to start with us watching each other. I don't know how you feel about that…"

"Yes! Yes, I think I like that," she said suddenly. He smiled as she pushed away from him, standing beside the bed. "I'll, umm, I'll get undressed and…"

"Get on the bed, baby. Sit against the headboard for me." She nodded, pulling the leggings down along with her panties. Turning her back to him, she pulled the sweater over her head and then unhooked the bra, setting her glasses on the night table. As she turned, her hands instinctively covered her breasts. Ace shook his head.

"Let me see, Charlie." She let her hands fall, and he drank her in. The small swell of her stomach, the full creamy thighs, and the auburn curls glistening with desire. Her breasts were heavy, big pink nipples standing at attention. Charlie crawled on the bed, leaning against the headboard.

"You-you have to get naked, Alex." He nodded, pulling off the t-shirt. His tattooed chest, carved muscles making her melt. Unbuckling his jeans, she heard them as they hit the floor, and then she looked up to see Alex in all his glory, long, thick, the big purple head wet with precum.

"This is way better than my books," she whispered. Alex laughed and nodded, stroking his cock.

"Touch yourself, honey," he said, looking at her. Charlie spread her legs wide and slid a finger between her folds, letting one glide inside. "That's it, baby. Play with your tits." She did as he asked, tweaking one nipple and letting a gasp slip from her lips.

"Oh God, Alex, this is so hot. Stroke yourself," she begged. "Does it feel good?"

"Better than ever," he growled. "Play with your clit, Charlie girl. Play with that beautiful nub." Charlie tweaked her own clit, rubbing it faster.

"I-I need to touch you. I need you to touch me. Can we?" she asked. Alex nodded, feeling a hot need to feel her skin beneath his fingers. Standing beside her, he let his free hand glide down her stomach and between her legs, his fingers finding the wetness he knew was there.

Charlie slowly reached out, touching his balls, feeling the weight of them in her hands, then her fingers gliding upward. Alex let her grip him and then placed his own hand over hers, stroking up and down.

"Oh God, Alex..." she moaned.

"Yea, baby, fuck, that's good. You feel good, Charlie..."

"Cum on me, Alex," she begged. "Please let me feel you on me." Alex nodded, jerking their hands together in rhythm, all the while keeping time with his own fingers inside her. As she bucked against him, her walls clenching around him, he felt the first burst of desire spill over her stomach. Charlie never let go, pumping him until every last drop was gone.

She started to remove her hand, but he held it around his still semi-hard cock. Smiling, she stroked him again and then turned, kneeling on all fours.

"D-do you think this is okay?" she asked. He could only nod at the sight of her pretty white ass in the air, her tits swinging beneath her. She inched forward, her hot breath at the tip of his cock, and for a moment, he thought he might panic, but when her sweet, soft lips wrapped around him, all Ace could think about was gripping her hair and fucking her mouth.

"Oh fuck, Charlie. Fuck, baby," he growled. She nodded as he pumped faster and harder, and when his hot load hit the back of her throat, Charlie swallowed. The first time she hadn't gagged, the first time she swallowed, and the first time she truly enjoyed sucking a dick.

Alex's eyes were glazed over with desire and heat, the need already building in his body once again.

"I need to taste you, Charlie," he said, crawling between her legs. "Open for me, precious." She did as he asked, waiting to feel the crushing, oppressive weight of her anxiety. Except it never came. What she felt instead was an intense need and desire. His hands played softly up her thighs, gently pushing her wider and wider. His thick hair tickled her skin.

Charlie arched up before he even touched his tongue to her body, just the presence of him so near and between her legs enough to bring her near the brink. He lay his big wide hand flat on her belly, his thumb massaging her clit.

"You taste so good, Charlie," he said, flicking his tongue between her lips. His hot breath hit her body, and Charlie nearly came out of her skin at the sensations flooding her. Alex's tongue was like a magic vibrator, in and out, wiggling, shaking against her.

"A-Alex, oh wow, I'm..."

"Do it, Charlie. Come for me, baby girl," he said against her lips. She felt the rush of desire flow from her body, and Alex moaned beneath her. He gave two quick, final licks and then stared up at her, his face flush with need. "Fuck, Charlie, that was perfect, baby."

"I-I can't believe we both did that. We got through it," she smiled. Alex nodded, leaning back on his heels. She looked down to see his big cock already hard again. "You have a beautiful penis, Alex. I should know. I write about them all the time."

Alex let out a big laugh, his head nodding toward her.

"You're pretty fucking hot yourself, Charlie girl. I want to feel you around me, Charlie. I've never... never gotten this far with a woman."

"I know. I-I mean, I have gotten this far... with a man, not a woman. I mean, never what we just did... never... but this usually is... mechanical," she blushed.

"Fuck that, honey. Nothing about us appears to be mechanical. Let me have you, Charlie. Will you, baby?"

"Yes, God, yes, please, Alex. Take me," she cried, reaching for him. Alex didn't hesitate, sliding his big cock inside her, filling her tight body, taking her for all she could stand.

It was nearly two a.m. by the time they'd finally exhausted themselves and showered. Alex realized if his dick was sore, her pussy was probably hurting as well.

"Are you sore? Hurting anywhere?" he asked.

"No, a little," she grinned, pulling closer to him. "It's the best kind of sore in my whole life, Alex. I need you to know that. I've never, and I do mean never, done any of that with a man."

"The oral?" he questioned, looking at her.

"No... no man ever... and I never... it was beautiful, Alex. Tasting you was the most wonderfully intimate thing I've ever done. The way you took control in our lovemaking was hot. I mean, beyond what even I could write about or dream about."

"Well, I think it only turned out that way because of my beautiful partner," he grinned. "Listen, Charlie, we both know that neither of us is very experienced, but I think together our discovery and exploration with our bodies makes this more magical, more extreme in some ways. We're not virgins, but we're not experienced either."

"Mmhmm," she said, nodding against his chest.

"You're tired, honey, sleep. Can I stay in here with you?"

"Yes, I mean, I hoped..."

"All I need to hear," he said, pulling the covers up over them.

"Alex?"

"Hmm?"

"Tomorrow night, do you think we could try out some things I'm writing about? I mean, I brought these toys, and I'm not sure if they'll work in the real world, and I..." Lips crashed against hers, and she gasped as he spread her legs again.

"Talk to me about your fucking sex scenes, honey, and I'm gonna want to take you again," he growled. Charlie giggled and opened wider for him.

"Good to know. So tomorrow night, we're good?" Alex growled in her ear, and Charlie laughed so loudly she thought the whole building heard her.

"Start taking notes, baby. I'm writing a new chapter."

CHAPTER EIGHTEEN

"Two fucking forty-five before you rabbits finally shut it down," said Hawk, grinning at Ace as he walked into the kitchen. Any other time and Ace would have blushed and run from the room. Today, he was feeling a bit prideful, maybe a little smug, and could only smile.

"Sorry, man. Not sorry," he said, grinning. "It was... unexpected."

"Brother, I could not be happier for you, truly, Ace," said Hawk, gripping his shoulder. "She's a nice woman and hot as fuck, so that helps things along. Really, I'm happy for you." Ace nodded, looking up to see Ghost and Zulu smiling at him as well.

"Two-forty-five? By my calculations, that's almost six hours from the time you left the dining room," said Ghost. "A man can get a lot done in six hours, Ace. You care to share any of your secrets, brother?"

"Yes, he can," said the younger man. "And, no, I don't. A gentleman never tells his secrets. None of you damn sure did."

"Alright, leave the boy alone," said Zulu. "Besides, according to Eagle, with whom you share a wall, you have a beautiful penis."

"Oh fuck," he moaned, rubbing his hands over his face.

"Yea, but it was a good fuck from what he heard," said Gunner.

The men broke into laughter, finally leaving Ace alone. They heard the thundering of footsteps racing down the stairs and waited to see who it was when Charlie came running in with her phone in her hand, shaking, her face a pale, ashen color.

"Charlie girl?" he said, standing. Charlie stretched out her phone to him.

"P-police... my house... my h-house burned down..." she cried. Ace took her phone and stepped into the hallway as Ghost pulled Charlie into a hug, soothing her with long back strokes.

"It's okay, Charlie. We'll figure this out. I promise you, we will find out what's going on and fix this for you," he said. Charlie sobbed against his chest, her head shaking back and forth. Grace, Bree, and Darby walked in, stunned to see Charlie in tears, immediately wondering what the hell Ace or one of the others had done to her.

"Charlie? Honey, what's wrong? What did these assholes say or do?" asked Grace.

"Thanks, honey," growled Ghost.

"N-nothing... my house b-burned down..." Grace pulled Charlie from Ghosts' arms and wrapped her into a hug, the girls all enveloping her into a group hug. Ace walked back into the room and grimaced at the sight of Charlie sobbing. It was killing him.

"What?" asked Charlie. "What did they say?"

"It was arson, honey. Someone used an accelerant of some sort. It was gone in a matter of minutes. You live pretty far out from the nearest fire department, so by the time they got there, there was nothing to save, Charlie. I'm sorry, baby." She nodded and left the comfort of Grace's arms to be folded into Ace's. The site of Ace comforting the woman made them all give a small smile, but it was laced with anger knowing that she was targeted.

"What am I going to do? I have nothing... nowhere to go."

"Yes, you do," said Ace, kissing her forehead. "You have me... us... all of us. You have this place, and we can build a place if you want, Charlie girl."

"Wh-what?" she looked up, shocked.

"I know it's fast, Charlie, but I've never met a woman like you... not someone I connected with immediately. I know it in my heart.

Seventy-two-fucking hours is all it took. I love you, Charlie. Stay." Charlie looked around the room at the smiling faces and then finally settled on the wise face of George. For some reason, his was the one she needed to ground her, to let her know she wasn't stuck in a dream or alternate reality.

"He loves you, honey. Nothin' to think about unless you don't love him."

"I do. I mean, I think I do. I... no, I do." Ace nodded, laughing at her. "How?"

"We don't question it around here," said Whiskey. "Shit sort of just happens like lightning in a bottle or something. You're family, Charlie, to all of us. Even if Ace wasn't in love with you, we'd ask you to stay." Nodding, she let her head rest against his chest, hugging him tightly.

"I have a home... with you," she said quietly.

"For as long as you'll put up with me, honey," he murmured against her hair, kissing the top of her head. His big hand splayed across her back, and Charlie felt truly safe for the first time in almost ten years.

"Okay, okay then," she said, smiling up at him. "Forever it is. Now what?"

"Now we keep you safe," said Ghost. "We find out who the hell set fire to your house and who your fan stalker is."

"Stalker?" said Grace, looking surprised. "Why would Charlie have a fan stalker? What do you do for a living? Are you an actress? No wait, I bet you're a singer, aren't you?" Damn, thought Ace. He really wanted to keep this surprise until Christmas, but no doubt he was going to have to tell the girls now. As the others filtered into the room, it was the perfect timing.

"So, Merry Christmas, everyone. Charlie was my Christmas surprise for all of you," he grinned, hugging her to him.

"Your Christmas surprise?" questioned Bree. Charlie smiled through her tears and stepped forward.

"My full name is Charlotte C. Tabor, or you know me as CC Robat." The loud squeals and screams nearly made Charlie run for the hills, but when the women finally settled, they pulled her in for hugs. Chattering a mile a minute, they were all spouting lines from her books, talking about their favorite scenes or characters, and all Charlie could do was smile, tears filling her eyes. She truly was home.

"Oh my God! Ace! I can't believe you did this for us," said Grace.

"I knew how much you all liked the books, how much you all got out of them," he said, blushing. "Although she didn't make it easy to find her, I know why now, but I couldn't find anything on this person, and there wasn't any contact information other than for her fan club. So, I wrote to the fan page of CC Robat and asked him... her to visit as a surprise for you guys, and she accepted. I didn't realize CC was a woman until we met a few days ago."

"I knew it was a woman!" said Gabi. "No man would understand a woman's body like that, know what a woman wants like that!" Charlie laughed, nodding her head.

"So, wait," said Grace, tilting her head, "you have a fan stalker?"

"Yes," said Charlie. "I'm worried it's the same one that kidnapped me years ago. I'm so sorry this followed me here. You all have children here. Oh God, maybe I should go."

"You're not leaving, Charlie. There is no place safer than right here with all these men. And don't think for a moment that we women can't hold our own. No, no, it's fine. Believe me, we all have a story," said Grace. "Why don't we sit for breakfast, and you tell us what's going on so everyone is aware. I know Ghost and Ace will make sure that the guys are doing their thing, but we girls aren't without resources as well."

"That's very kind of you all, but right now, I have nothing other than what I brought with me. I have no additional clothing, no shoes, my books... all my books are gone..."

"We'll replace anything we can, honey," said Ace, kissing her temple. "For now, let's get you fed. We can contact your insurance provider and start the process on that end. The police and fire department in the Outer Banks will take a few days to fully investigate and send over photos, then we can go from there. For now, eat." He leaned closer, whispering in her ear.

"We have another long night ahead."

CHAPTER NINETEEN

As the boys all left the room, the girls huddled closer around

Charlie to lend comfort but also to hear her whole story.

"So," smiled Gabi, "you and Ace?"

"Oh, wow, you guys really do stick together, don't you?" she

grinned.

"Honey, let me tell you something," said Bree. "These men are

the epitome of alpha male, over-protective, hovering, loving, sweet, sexy

as shit men." The women all giggled a bit at her statement, smiling and

nodding in agreement.

"When I came to Club Steel, it was really to meet with Grace. She

was recovering from her own trauma, and that's how I met Doc. He was

an overbearing asshole at the time, but damn, he was handsome. Tall,

muscular, wow, my girly-bits are screaming. Anyway, he protected me

like no man in my entire life had. Your man, Ace, he did something for me

that allows me to live without fear, to live in peace. He made sure my

stepfather would never touch me again. That man out there, the one who

couldn't stand to touch anyone... until you, that is... took it upon himself

to make sure that man never touched anyone again."

"Oh, wow," whispered Charlie.

"All of these men are sort of in that same frame," said Grace. "I was beaten and nearly killed by my ex-husband... after he'd already killed my twin daughters on their graduation day and my parents."

"Oh, my God, Grace," she said, reaching for the woman's hand.

"No, don't feel bad for me, honey. It was tragic, no doubt about it. But what would have made it more tragic was if I hadn't met Ghost. If I had up and left... run when things got scary. That man changed my world. He gave me a gift... two gifts," she sniffed, laughing, "two precious gifts that I thought I would never have." Charlie nodded, looking at Gabi.

"Oh me? Well, I saved Zulu when he was shot during a mission. I stayed with him in his room. There was a hurricane, and all the patients had been moved, but I stayed with him. I fell in love with a man I barely knew, and when I got back to the hospital after a few days off, he was gone. Fifteen years later, I found myself in some trouble, hurt, and looked him up and came here. He remembered me."

"She's being modest," said Taylor, "he had been dreaming of her for fifteen years, not even realizing she was real."

"That's true," she smiled. "I got pregnant almost right away and gave birth to those two giant babies. Lord, how I love that man, crave him… every day. Ace helped us track down the man causing all the problems I was having."

"Same," said Kat. "The man I was raised to believe was my father was actually my uncle. A Russian crime boss. Whiskey kept me safe, fought for me, faced five mob families for me, and in the end, made me feel like the most beautiful, amazing woman on the planet. He's supported me as I took the bar, and now, we're having our first baby."

Charlie looked at the other women as each told their story, the love for their men so evident, the love for Ace clearly written on their faces as they described him always assisting.

"So, tell us your story, Charlie," smiled Grace. "This is a judgment-free zone here, honey. No one cares about anything other than how you feel about Ace." Charlie smiled at the women and nodded. She told the story of how she'd been kidnapped at her book signing, the pressures placed on her by her publisher, and how she'd left as soon as she got Ace's letter.

"It's such a mess," she sniffed. "I thought I could get away for a week or two, do some writing, and help out this sweet man who wanted to give you all a gift. Now, my house is burned to the ground. I have nothing left. I have no publisher, which is okay, really. I just feel so lost."

"Honey, we all feel lost now and then," said Bree. "The thing is, you've got a man willing to help lead you away from all that. He's standing in that other room, speaking to all those alpha-male, leather-wearing, tattoo-covered badasses, telling them what he's going to do to ensure your safety." Charlie smiled at the description of the men.

"I don't know how this happened. I walked in the door three nights ago, dropped everything on the floor, and that man... he was so handsome, his blue eyes, those lips..." she said, trailing off as she touched her own. "I write erotic romance for a living and last night... last night was the first time I'd ever actually experienced it." Eyes went wide in the room as the women looked at her.

"You were you a virgin?" asked Taylor.

"Oh, no, no, not a virgin. I was just inexperienced. I've only had two long-term relationships before, and they weren't all that great. Both men were, well, honestly terrible in bed. James, my editor, he would get naked, rub his dick for a bit, and then lay there basically telling me to climb on."

"Holy shit, that sucks," said Darby.

"Yep," she nodded, "and then he told me I was hum-drum in bed. Even threatened to tell the world that the romance writer was a terrible lover. I think it's why I started writing. I had all these ideas in my head about how men and women should be together. I just never got to experience it. Until last night with Ace."

"What a piece of shit this James is!" yelled Kat. Charlie laughed at the tiny woman.

"Yes, he is that. Ace, though, I mean, I worried we wouldn't be able to touch. It took me a long time to touch James. But with Ace, I was begging him to touch me... and... and he did. Lord, he did in so many ways, so many right ways. It was amazing." Her face flushed a bright pink, and Charlie realized that for the first time in her life, she was having girl chat, like real, substantial girl chat with a group of women she admired.

"That's awesome," giggled Bella. "I mean, Ace is so sweet, and I know he struggled with touching people, but maybe you were his muse or something. Like, once he touched you, the spell was broken. It's romantic."

"Alright, ladies, we have our mission," said Grace, standing. "Everyone, laptops. It's time to do some retail therapy for our new friend. Charlie, don't buy anything. We will purchase everything in our names so that nothing is traced to your card or this shipping address."

"I never even thought of that," she said, smiling.

"We got it, girl. You can pay us back later, no worries. Let's get you all the clothes you need, anything at all. Ladies, start your engines!"

CHAPTER TWENTY

Ace finished speaking to the insurance company and then connected them to the fire department's investigator. It took him nearly an hour to explain to the agent that there was no way in hell Charlie was leaving her current location to meet him anywhere. When the agent finally understood the gravity of the situation, he agreed that he didn't need to meet with Charlie face-to-face.

Ace turned in his chair to see Eagle sitting at the conference table deep in thought, leaning over his laptop. Eagle and Hawk, Tyran "Ty" and Ryan respectively, were twenty-seven-year-old twin brothers who also happened to both be prolific Marine snipers. Where Hawk was brash, boisterous, a constant joker and man-whore, Eagle was quieter, more reserved, careful with his selection of words, and seemed willingly to follow his brother. What Ace figured out long ago, though, was that Eagle followed his brother to keep him out of trouble.

When Hawk announced that he was joining the Marines, Eagle followed to ensure his brother didn't get killed. When Hawk wanted to pursue a woman, and she had friends with her, Eagle would tag along so he could get the girl. When Hawk wanted a threesome, or sometimes even a foursome, Eagle would agree. Although maybe that wasn't all for his brother.

Where Hawk often said things that set Ace's teeth on fire, Eagle rarely said anything, and when he did, it was well thought out, intelligent, and insightful. It wasn't that Ace didn't like Hawk, but given the choice, he would rather be in a closed room with Eagle.

"You're not gonna like what I found, brother," said Eagle, turning to stare at Ace.

"Damn, I was afraid you were going to say that. Should I bring in the others?" asked Ace. Eagle nodded, and Ace quickly sent a text message summoning them all to the meeting room, including the women.

Everyone squeezed into the big room, and Ghost smiled, suddenly realizing that they were running out of space, and to him, that was a good sign. He looked at the smiling faces of his teammates and their wives, some nestled securely on their husbands' laps, and felt pride for having created exactly what they set out to do.

"Eagle has some information that everyone needs to hear, especially you, honey," he said, pulling Charlie into his arms as if it were the most natural thing in the world.

"Athenaeum House of Publishing or AHP has been in business for about forty years now," he started. "They are a family-owned company."

"Wait, family-owned?" asked Charlie. "I was told that they were owned by an investment group."

"Yea, the group is the family," said Eagle. "Wanda DiBenedetto is the daughter of the original founder."

"Oh my God, how could I not have known that?" whispered Charlie. Ace pulled her into his body tighter, rubbing her shoulders with firm hands, soothing her.

"They kept it pretty well hidden, Charlie. The company was only making ends meet until they brought on a new author ten years ago— Charlotte C. Tabor or CC Robat. Your first book published by APH brought in more than thirty million in revenues. It only got better from there for them. They literally laid all their eggs in one basket, you. When you refused to do book signings, they started bringing on other authors, and most have done fairly well, but believe me when I say this, you are their golden goose."

"I-I don't know what to say. I mean, I knew that my books brought in a lot of revenue for them, but I honestly never paid attention to who else they were representing. I just assumed it was a lot of people, not a few." Ghost nodded and then gave a quick nod to Eagle to continue.

"Wanda seems to have a bit of a gambling problem. She bets on everything from the ponies to ball games. She owes some people a lot of money. James Walsh is her nephew."

"I think I'm going to be sick," whispered Charlie as she wrapped her arms around her stomach. Doc stood and ordered Hawk to get a glass of ginger ale. He reached for the waste basket, gently setting it beside her and then pushing her head down between her knees.

"Take some deep breaths, honey," he said softly. A few minutes later, a few sips later, and she was ready to continue.

"H-how did I not know?"

"They didn't share a last name, didn't tell anyone from what it seems. In fact, it seems it's what APH was really good at, not telling anyone anything. When you were kidnapped, Charlie, do you remember any discussions around problems with your book?"

"Problems? N-no, I mean, my books always sold well. I remember there was another author coming out with something similar at the time. They'd even signed a movie deal. Wanda and James were really pushing for me to do the same, but I just didn't want that." Eagle nodded, frowning.

"They were pushing for it because sales were down, and they needed something to get them back up. Kidnapping you was the best way to put your name back in the spotlight."

"Wh-what? You think... you think they..."

"I'm almost positive, Charlie," said Eagle. "The sales were way down from the quarter before. You were slowing down on the book signings. People just weren't talking as much. After the kidnapping, your sales went through the roof. I don't think their intention was to ever hurt you, but only to gain publicity for your name... for the books."

"But..."

"You angered them when you decided to switch pen names. Now? Yea, well, now, they're in a similar situation. Their financials are a disaster, and if the investors come in and look at the books, they're going to find that Wanda has been skimming off the top and James too. In the last two years, collectively, they've bought and sold at least ten homes, always going bigger. They each own four cars. They've taken trips to

Europe, Asia, anywhere and everywhere and written it off as a company expense."

"But why threaten me? If my books are making them money, what do they get out of this?" she asked. Ace looked down at her and smiled.

"If they could convince you to do book signings, they could actually arrange for another kidnapping, and this time it would be CC Robat, not Charlotte Tabor. They would be making money off your misery once again, babe. If you died, then they still make money because people would be clamoring for your books."

"And I would bet that James would be churning out books under my name, and they would sell them as 'lost' works, maybe for years to come. I can't believe this. The people I thought were my friends..."

"So, how does this tie into the stalker?" asked Whiskey.

"I think James and Wanda are the stalkers," said Ace. "I've had an inkling all along, but what Eagle found only solidifies that for me. I think if we set a trap, pull out the stalker, we can stop this."

"How do we do that?" asked Charlie.

"Simple," smiled Eagle, "we invite them to dinner."

CHAPTER TWENTY-ONE

Fanboy365, I'm not sure what you want from me. I have no idea what chapters or scenes you're referring to. I want you to leave me alone, and if the only way to do that is to meet you, then I'm willing. I'm taking some time off in the mountains. If you wish to discuss these chapters or scenes, meet me at a restaurant called Club Steel on the 23rd at 6 pm.

"Is that good?" she asked, turning to Ace. He pushed her glasses up the bridge of her nose and placed a kiss on her adorable tip.

"Perfect, baby, let's see if we get a response, and if they do respond, I can tell you for certain if it's them."

"And if it's not them?" she asked. Eagle looked at the woman, his heart feeling for her.

"If it's not them, we'll still follow through. Your stalker will be gone, and we'll deal with Wanda and James separately, but believe me, Charlie, I think these two are your stalker." Eagle folded his arms across his chest, waiting to see if Fanboy365 would respond.

"I still can't believe they would do this to me. Although it makes sense the way James treated me," she said, shaking her head. Eagle looked up with a cocked brow and frown. Ace turned to mirror his expression.

"What way he treated you?" asked Ace.

"Like... like I was a commodity, not a person. I told you..." she blushed, looking at Eagle and somehow knew it was okay to speak freely with him in the room. "he was terrible in the bedroom... always like it was such a chore. He would... he would strip and rub himself to get hard and then lay there basically telling me to go ahead and climb on. I always felt dirty and ashamed when I was done."

"Damn, baby, I hate that he made you feel that way," said Ace, pulling her in for a hug. "You're a beautiful, sexy, intelligent woman, Charlie. Any man who didn't see that wasn't worth your time or energy. I'm damn glad he was too stupid to see it."

"I'd have to agree, Charlie," said Eagle in a serious tone. "My brother may say things more openly than I do, but I would agree with Ace completely. You're beautiful and intelligent, and believe me, in my head, intelligence always wins. My brother tends to go for the blonde bimbo type, but then again, he's somewhat of a bimbo himself."

Charlie laughed at Eagle as he winced with his own words.

"Thank you, Eagle. Really, I appreciate…" Her words were interrupted by the telltale ping of a new message coming in.

Finally, you understand the need for us to meet. Wear something sexy. I'll be there at 6.

"Fucker," growled Ace under his breath. "Alright, let's let the others know to be ready. For now, why don't you and I go for a walk, honey, get some fresh air?"

"Sounds perfect," she said, taking his hand. As they made their way to the door, Charlie turned, placing a kiss on Eagle's cheek. "Thank you, Ty, for everything." He casually nodded as they walked out and then touched his cheek. Ace was damn lucky he didn't find Charlie first. She was exactly the kind of woman he wanted. Unlike his brother, Eagle didn't want silicone tits, bleached blonde hair, and overfilled lips. He wanted a natural woman, a mature woman with her head on straight, and the fact that she might be a little older was a huge fucking turn-on.

"She's great, isn't she?" said Hawk, his big body leaning against the doorframe. "Maybe we should plot to steal her from Ace." Eagle knew his brother was joking, but he'd had enough.

"Not funny," he said, closing his laptop. "Don't you get tired of chasing pussy, Ry? Doesn't it ever get old for you? Having empty-headed blondes sucking your dick, and you don't even remember their names? Don't you want something more? Something like that?" he said, pointing down the hall.

Hawk looked at his brother, frowning. Standing straight, he shoved his hands in his pockets, staring at Eagle.

"I was fucking joking. What the hell is wrong with you?" he asked.

"Nothing, nothing at all." Eagle shoved past his brother and headed upstairs to his own room, leaving Hawk with his mouth open, his mind scattered, and if he admitted it, his heart hurt just a little.

CHAPTER TWENTY-TWO

Their walk didn't last long as the snow began falling with a vengeance. Rare snow thunder and lightning filled the sky as they ran into the barn. Ace asked if he could meet her later in the dining room, claiming he had some things to get done for work. She agreed, knowing that she also needed to get some things done. A while later, they opened their room doors at the same time, smiling, and walked hand-in-hand downstairs, meeting the others in the dining room.

"This might play well for us tomorrow night," said Ghost. "With the holiday and now the storm, folks won't venture out for dinner."

The smells of the holidays filled the barn. Orange, cinnamon, pine, and nutmeg filtered throughout the restaurant and even up to the living spaces. George fixed a big meal for everyone while the children played with the holiday decorations. Eagle sat at one end of the table. Hawk at the other, uncharacteristically separated.

Whiskey frowned, seeing the two brothers apart. In the seven years they'd known them, never had they seen them apart for more than a few minutes. Something was happening, and he wasn't sure whether it was good or bad.

"I know it's not Christmas," said Charlie, standing at the table, "but I have a gift for all of you. When I received Alex's letter to come here, I thought I would be able to write a little. I was mistaken. I've written a lot." Nervous laughter drifted down the table as all eyes turned back to Charlie.

"I didn't use anyone's names or any important information about your location or who you are, but Alex did inspire me to write. Some of my best writing is done in the middle of the night, and that's what I've done." She pulled out the packets from her bag and handed them down the table. "I've started writing something new. Something for each of you, with each of you. This is only the beginning, the first fifteen chapters, but I hope you like it."

"Oh my God," whispered Grace with a tear. "You've written a book... for us... about us?"

"It's not exactly about you, more inspired by you," she smiled. "I hope it, ummm, inspires all of you... tonight." Her crimson blush told them all what she meant, and the men all cheered as the women silently did the same.

Later in their rooms, each couple read a few chapters to one another, never getting very far before they were on top of each other, inside one another, touching one another. Charlie captured them perfectly in the words and the descriptions.

"Are you ready to read?" asked Charlie. Alex was seated against the headboard, naked with only the sheet pulled to his hips. The deep vee of his muscles was already sending tingles down Charlie's body. He nodded at her. Charlie started reading.

His body was so beautifully sculpted, Caroline thought it couldn't possibly be real. This man couldn't possibly want her. The curve of his muscles, chiseled to perfection, the tattoos seemingly melted into his skin. The way his dark hair brushed his forehead, the same hair surrounding that perfectly erotic cock...

"God, Charlie," he moaned as his cock stood straight up, telling her he loved the words.

"Don't interrupt," she smiled.

... that perfectly erotic cock, his big purple head screaming for her lips. Caroline bent down and kissed it, flicking her tongue out to taste his juice... the juice meant for her. Her delicate hands massaged his thighs as

she lowered her mouth to him, feeling him hit the back of her throat. She could feel her own desires building, the need to seat herself on him...

"Charlie, if you don't fucking stop and get on top of me, I'm not going to be held responsible for what I do, baby," he growled. Charlie looked up, seeing that beautiful cock, just as she'd described it, begging for her attention. She pulled his t-shirt over her head, something she'd enjoyed wearing every night they were together, tossing it to the floor. Setting the pages aside, she crawled up his body, straddling his thighs. Positioning his head at her opening, she slowly let her body fall onto him until she couldn't move any further.

"Oh, Alex, you're so perfect," she whispered as her hips ground against him, rubbing her sweet clit against him. Alex gripped her tits, taking a nipple between his teeth and tugging. His big hands moved up her back to her shoulders and pushed down, forcing her to take his entire length. Charlie gasped at the invasion to her body and then smiled, pushing her hair from her face.

Alex reached up, gently removing her glasses and then kissing her.

"There she is. I want to see those beautiful eyes, Charlie girl. I want to see them when I tell you I love you. I want you in my life forever,

Charlie. Be my wife, Charlie girl. Marry me, have my babies," he said, cupping her face with both hands.

"A-Alex..." tears filled her eyes as she kissed him, "yes, yes, I'll be your wife." He reached into the bedside table and pulled out a blue velvet box, opening it slowly.

"Good, I'd hate to have to return this," he said, sliding it onto her finger. "Now, fuck me, Charlie. Any way you want, baby, but let me have that sweet pussy of yours."

Charlie nodded, rocking back and forth, gripping his shoulders as the huge diamond sparkled, winking at her. Her tits bounced against his chest, the nipples rubbing his warm, sensitive skin. Each time they touched, Charlie felt the sizzling desire pulse through her body.

Alex reached up, gripping all that beautiful hair in his hands, and pulled her head back. Latching onto her neck, he sucked and kissed, his own need building with a fury. Finally, unable to control himself, he flipped Charlie to her back and relentlessly pumped inside her as she wrapped her legs around his waist.

"Yes, yes, Alex..." she cried out. Alex covered her mouth with his own, tasting her, filling her with his desire until they both shuddered with their orgasm, finally slowing. Alex didn't move, only shifting his weight slightly off of her as his cock began hardening again inside her.

"That's at least six times without a condom, Alex. Are you trying to trap me into marriage?" she grinned.

"Baby, anything I can do to get you to stay, you'd better believe I'm going to do it. You're mine, Charlie. My fucking woman and I will do anything for you. If I've put a baby or two in your belly, I'm damn sure happy about it." She smiled, kissing him as she shook her head.

"You're such a dichotomy, Alex. One minute, you're this genius computer guy with the vocabulary of a literary professor, and the next minute, you're this hard-as-nails, rough, alpha male."

"Is that bad, baby?" he asked.

"No, it's the hottest, sexiest thing I've ever seen. You turn me on in so many ways, Alex. I can't even wrap my head around how all this happened, but I know it was meant to be. You are meant to be mine, and I am meant to be yours. There is nothing, and I do mean nothing, that I don't love about you. I hope you put a baby in my belly... or two," she smiled. "I'm thirty-seven. I want children, and I want more than one... with you... so we need to get started."

"Agreed, now open those beautiful legs so I can fuck you again, Charlie. I need you, baby, need you bad."

"Gladly," she said, kissing him. "We didn't finish our story."

"You're right, baby, because our story doesn't end. It keeps going… together."

"Wow," she gasped as he thrust inside her, "maybe you should be the writer." Alex laughed, biting down on one big pink nipple as he moved slowly inside her, feeling their previous juices coat him.

"No way, honey. You write it. I'll gladly play it out."

"Deal."

CHAPTER TWENTY-THREE

Charlie nervously twisted her napkin in her lap, staring at the bowl of soup in front of her. George was behind the bar, dressed like an eighty-year-old incapable of doing anything other than pour beer. Charlie knew it was a ruse, but no one else would know by looking at him.

Behind her, Eagle, Skull, and Gunner were laughing about something on the television above their seats, while seated at another table were Ghost, Grace, Zulu, and Gabi. She knew that outside were the other men, safely tucked away from view, waiting on Fanboy365 to show himself.

What if he wasn't James. What if it was someone else, someone far more dangerous? She couldn't even contemplate the kind of danger that might walk through that door, but then again, she'd learned over the last week that the men who lived here were their own kind of danger. She smiled as the sweet sounds of her man filtered into her ear.

We've got you, Charlie girl. Nothin' gonna happen to you, baby. I love you.

Charlie felt the tears filling her eyes and willed them back, not wanting to give any indication that someone was speaking to her.

Although she expected it, she nearly gasped when Wanda and James walked in the door of the restaurant. Fortunately, that also forced a surprised expression to her face.

"Hello, Charlotte," said Wanda, sneering at her. "You've been difficult to find these last two weeks."

"Wh-what are you doing here? Wanda? James? Why are you here?" she asked.

"You really are stupid, aren't you, Charlotte?" said James. "I'm fanboy365, always have been."

"Y-you kidnapped me all those years ago... the two of you? You kept me in that box!" she nearly yelled.

"Quit sniveling, you coward!" hissed Wanda. "I tried to tell you what you needed to do, but no, you wouldn't listen. James even tried rewriting some of that drivel you put out, but you wouldn't listen to him either. We had no choice! You and your pathetic fear of people!" The old Charlotte would have crumbled in tears, terror overcoming her, but the new Charlotte... Charlie was fearless.

"You despicable, evil bitch!" she spat. "You and your pathetically inept nephew. Yes, I know... are nothing but a couple of conniving, no-talent hacks. You thought you could drive my career? You thought you would make the decisions around my life? You are nothing. I will not publish another word with your name on it. I will not publish another book with the label of APH."

"You were a pathetic lay, Charlie," grinned James as if somehow that might stab a knife in her gut, instead only making her feel proud.

"Pathetic, you say?" Charlie smiled as the men slowly made their way up behind the two individuals. "I'd say pathetic describes you and your lifeless dick, James. Any man who has to rub it out himself before attempting to satisfy his woman is pretty sad. You see, I've learned a few things in the last few weeks. One is that I don't need either of you. I never did. Two is that I'm not to blame for the hum-drum in the bedroom. I've learned that I'm quite a vixen in the bed when my partner has a cock worth riding and sucking."

James's face turned beet red, his fists clenching as he started to lean toward Charlie. She never moved, though, making him even more wary as to why she didn't back up. Then he knew. He understood her newfound strength. He felt it. A big hand squeezing his shoulder with such ferocity, he was certain a bone would break beneath the grip.

"That's right, limp dick. I'm the hot cock she's been fucking, and I gotta tell you, you give men a bad name because that woman is fucking hot in the bedroom. Top that with the fact that she's sexy as fuck, brilliant, and is one hellacious writer, and I've found me a winner."

"Wh-who are you?" he squirmed.

"Me? Oh, I'm the man who is going to marry this beautiful woman and give her as many children as she wants while she writes all the books her little mind can think up. Self... published."

"You can't do this!" yelled Wanda. "We'll sue you for breach of contract!"

"Actually," said Kat, walking up with Whiskey. "I've reviewed the contract, and it's unethical as well as contains clauses which are either illegal or wouldn't hold water in a court of law. So, please go ahead and sue. We'll see you in court, prove you were behind the kidnapping, stalking, and attempts to destroy Charlie's career, and I will rip apart your publishing firm and own it when I'm through."

"Fucking hot as shit, baby," said Whiskey, kissing her temple.

"Who the hell are you?" growled James.

"Me? I'm her attorney, Katarina English." Wanda swallowed, seeing the crowd of people surrounding Charlotte. Her meek, pushover finally found her voice, damn her. All this time, she'd been able to control her, and now in her most desperate hour, the little bitch found her nerve. That's alright. There was still one more option. Wanda reached in her bag, pulling out the small pistol, ready to wave it at Charlie, when a massive paw gripped her wrist so tightly, the crunching of bone echoed.

"I don't think so, bitch," said George. "Not on my watch." Charlie smiled at George as he winked at her. The front doors opened, and Sheriff Webb walked in with three deputies.

"This your stalker and kidnapper?" he asked.

"Yes, sir," said Charlie. "We have it all recorded. They kidnapped me ten years ago and were plotting to do the same here."

"No, no, you can't..." gasped Wanda, holding her wrist to her chest.

"I can, and I will," said Charlie. "I'm certain the investors will be removing you and your family from APH. It will have new ownership but never fear, I won't be using them or any other publishing house again."

The sheriff cuffed both Wanda and James and headed toward the front door.

"Oh, and Wanda? I'll be doing a book signing tomorrow. I think I'll be turning over a new leaf." Wanda could be heard screaming as she was led into the night, but it was Charlie who squealed with delight as Ace picked her up, twirling her in his arms. "We did it!"

"Yea, baby, you did it. You were so brave, so perfect, honey," he said, kissing her.

"Well done, Charlie!" said Kat, hugging the other woman. "That was awesome to see their faces when you confronted them. I'm so glad we could help you with this."

"It's over," she whispered against Alex's chest. "It's done. I can live life now... our life."

"Our life, baby. Let's get to livin' it."

CHAPTER TWENTY-FOUR

Charlie did the surprise book signing at the Page Turner, generating more sales in one day than Darby had in the entire months of November and December combined. After four hours, she had to shove people out the door and lock it to keep fans away. Charlie was grateful but also felt excited that she'd made it through the event, promising Darby she would do exclusive signings when she launched the next book.

Christmas Eve with four children, even little ones who didn't quite understand, was more than most of the guys had ever experienced before. Tango, Skull, and Razor were putting together the mini motorcycles they'd designed for each of the kids, the little ones getting safety seats with belts and training wheels, while Calla's was a gleaming pink and white with flaming red hearts down the side in the shape of flames.

The dollhouse designed and created by George sat on the table, the small furnishings filling its rooms. The boys all getting carved rocking chairs. Presents were piled up under the tree while Hawk and Eagle were outside making sleigh and reindeer tracks.

When it was finished, they stood back admiring their work, smiling at one another. The Christmas music filtered through the restaurant, and without even knowing they'd done it, each man grabbed his girl and started swaying, dancing quietly to the music as the others watched, soaking up their love. Tomorrow it would be loud and noisy and chaotic once again, but tonight, it was quiet and peaceful.

In the privacy of their own homes, the couples gave one another their presents, finished reading Charlie's pages, making sweet love until the early morning hours.

The next morning, when the children were done ripping through their own presents, everyone made their way to the barn to tear into the other gifts. While the kids played with their new toys and the table was set for their holiday meal, Charlie pulled Alex upstairs to their room. He damn sure didn't argue, and when she stripped to reveal a bright red lace bustier, garter, thigh-high hose, and no panties, he nearly came in his jeans.

"I couldn't wait," she said breathlessly, "I need you now." Alex was happy to oblige, taking her against the wall, over the sofa, in the bed, and then finally in the shower. When they stepped back into the restaurant, they were getting the evil eye for making dinner wait. Charlie blushed, but it was Alex who grinned like a Cheshire cat, nodding at the men.

"A toast," said Ghost. "To our growing family once again, to three new babies coming in the spring, maybe more." He winked at Charlie, who laughed.

"I wanted this," he said, nodding at his teammates. "I always wanted this—family, brothers, teammates for life."

"For life!" came the chorus. Alex leaned over and whispered in Charlie's ear.

"I love you, Charlie girl."

"Love you more, Alex."

EXCERPT from HAWK & EAGLE

New Year's Eve. Another fucking year staring at my idiot brother doing stupid shit thought Eagle. His twin, Hawk, was on the other side of the big restaurant/bar flirting with three women, all a little tipsy, all a little under-dressed, and all eye-fucking him and his twin.

"Not this shit again," he muttered. Eagle liked sex as much as the next man, but his brother was on a whole other level. He often fucked two or three women at once, even getting his twin in on the action, not that he needed help getting action. Eagle wasn't opposed, but there were only so many times you could see your brother's dick driving into some girl and then having her want the same thing from him.

Deciding he couldn't sit and watch the show happening with his twin, he stepped outside in the frigid night air for a breather. Times like this, he wished he smoked, but then again, that's exactly what had killed their father. Emphysema was a bitch, and when you're not even sixty, it's even worse. He kicked a huge pile of snow, causing flakes and snowballs to go flying through the air.

"What did that snow ever do to you?" said the melodic voice behind him. He turned, ready to give a smart-ass response, instead seeing the most luscious creature he'd ever laid eyes on. At six-foot-two, Eagle

and his brother were both tall. His nearly two hundred and ten pounds of

muscle was something he prided himself in, working out every day.

This woman was probably five-feet-nine, her blunt-cut, mahogany

hair kissing her jaw as she moved. She had full red lips, enhanced by

nothing, it seemed, other than genetics. Her eyes were huge, almost too

big for her face, almost. They were the color of sea glass, green and blue

combined, fringed in thick black lashes.

"Sorry," he said, staring at her, "did I get you?"

"No, I'm safe from the snow monster," she said, grinning. "I'm

Tinley."

"Eagle, ummm, Tyran or Ty, but my teammates call me Eagle," he

said, suddenly feeling flushed. She smiled again, nodding up at him.

"Those snow piles can be real little shits," she grinned.

"Yea, hey, you wanna go inside and have a drink?" he asked.

"Oh, I'd love to, but I'm waiting on..." she looked up as a woman

walked toward her. She had the same mahogany hair, only longer, same

tall body, her eyes a shade closer to blue than green. "There she is. Ty, this is my daughter, Keegan. Keegan, this is Ty." You could have pushed

Eagle over with a feather. Her daughter?

"Hi there," she said with a huge infectious smile. "Way to go,

Mom! He's hot."

"Keegan," said her mother under her breath. "I'm sorry, my

daughter doesn't often find her manners or her filter." Eagle couldn't

help but laugh.

"I think I know what you mean. I have a twin brother inside who

is exactly like that." Keegan's eyes grew wide as she looked the man up

and down.

"A twin!? Yes! Let's go, handsome. Introduce me to your

brother," said Keegan, storming through the doors. Tinley bit her lower

lip and shook her head.

"I'm really sorry. She's... assertive," said her mother. Eagle could

not get over the fact that the woman in front of him was the mother of a

girl old enough to drink. She was stunning, and his dick was definitely

taking note.

"Assertive can be good. What I want to know is whether or not

you'll let me buy you that drink."

"Oh, listen, you're adorable. Really, handsome, sexy... shit," she mumbled, nervously nibbling on her bottom lip, "I mean, you're very good looking, and obviously, you could have any young woman you want in that room, and I bet there are a lot of young women in that room who might like you, and I'm forty years old, and I'm sure that's a lot older than you, and I haven't been with a man in almost fifteen years, and you didn't need to hear that, and oh damn, I'm messing this up." Eagle let a big grin slip from his sexy lips and looked down at her.

"You're not messing anything up, Tinley. A drink, one drink."

"Okay, one drink."

OTHER BOOKS BY MARY KENNEDY YOU MIGHT ENJOY!

REAPER Security Series
Erin's' Hero
Lauren's Warrior
Lena's' Mountain
Sara's' Chance
Mary's Angel
Kari's Gargoyle
Rachelle's Savior
Adele's Heart
Tori's' Secret
Finding Lily
Montana Rules
Savannah Rain
Gray Skies
My First Choice
Three Wishes
Second Chances
One Day at a Time
When You Least Expect It
Missing Hearts
Trail of Love

Steel Patriots MC Series
Ghost – Book One
Doc – Book Two
Whiskey – Book Three
Zulu – Book Four
Gunner – Book Five
Tango – Book Six
Razor – Book Seven

My SEAL Boys (connections to the REAPER Series)
Ian
Noa
Carter
Lars
Trevor
Fitz
Chris
O'Hara

Strange Gifts Series
Dark Visions
Dark Medicine
Dark Flame

ABOUT THE AUTHOR

Mary Kennedy is the mother of two adult children, has an amazing son-in-law, and is grandmother to two beautiful grandsons. She works full-time at a job she loves, and writing is her creative outlet. She lives in Texas and enjoys traveling, reading, and cooking. Her passion for assisting veterans and veteran causes comes from a strong military family background. Mary loves to hear from her readers and encourages them to join her mailing list, as she'll keep you up-to-date on new releases at https://insatiableink.squarespace.com. You can also join her Facebook page at Insatiable Ink.

Dear Readers,

I love hearing from you and encourage you to visit my website Insatiable Ink. Leave me know your thoughts and ideas on new books or expanding on characters. It's also a safe space to give your own feelings, like those of the characters. I love reading about how you relate to the stories because as we all know, there's a little of each of them within us.

I look forward to hearing from you and hope you enjoy other books in my collections.

Explore... and enjoy!

www.ingramcontent.com/pod-product-compliance
Lightning Source LLC
Chambersburg PA
CBHW011435170626
46808CB00010B/3174